Brittney
My
Love
Cindy Preston

Every Secret Thing

A Novel

By

Cynthia Marlee Preston

This book is a work of fiction. Places, events, and situations in this story are purely fictional. Any resemblance to actual persons, living or dead, is coincidental.

© 2002 by Cynthia Marlee Preston.
All rights reserved.

No part of this book may be reproduced, stored in a retrieval system, or transmitted by any means, electronic, mechanical, photocopying, recording, or otherwise, without written permission from the author.

ISBN: 1-4033-2472-7 (Paperback)
ISBN: 1-4033-2471-9 (e-book)

This book is printed on acid free paper.

Synopsis

At age 41, Patrick Cutter's gangster street life is over and Terry Onstad's rich suburban housewife life dies in a divorce. They have both moved into the Minneapolis inner-city and their lives are about to collide as they meet at a suburban carwash where Terry's 15 year old daughter works for Patrick Cutter. After discovering that they live close to each other in Minneapolis, Terry offers Cutty rides home from work when she comes to pick up her daughter.

Getting acquainted through conversations in the car and getting to know one another by sharing experiences they find that two strangers from completely different worlds are able to merge into a relationship that encompasses love, understanding, and adventure, and transcends the trappings of worldly systems to discover the spiritual truth that unites them.

When they find themselves each losing a loved one to the streets, it's time for Cutty to investigate the situation. Cutty goes back to the streets to find his brother's murderer and Terry gets pulled into the mystery, intrigue and reality of the hustler's world.

Dedication

This book is dedicated to Cleophus (Bo) McCalister 1965-2001 and to the family, Mavis Vickers, Johnnie and Vernon McCalister, Samantha Olson, Chris Nordahl, Jamie and Derrick Hogan, Lory Giddings, Tasha Huffman, Joyce Hustad, Laurie Salin, Jermaine Mimms, Mark Jesinowski and of course, Patrick Sr., Patrick Jr. Phillip, Stevie, Inna, Angelina, Nicolle, Isaiah, Sophia, LP, and Elijah, without whom life would be so dull!

A special thank you to my mother and father, Ruth and Earl Herring, for never giving up on me. They inspire me to achieve. And they forgive EVERYTHING! I love you both, very much. Pam, Vicki, Bobbi and David, my sisters and brother, my family, and my roots. You are my best friends of all.

Bo McCalister, my brother-in-law, who was killed by a gun last April, inspired this story. Rest in peace, Bo, and God Bless You.

Forward

Hate groups spring from unchecked self-righteousness. Several of the major institutions of the world are set up to keep self-righteousness in check: the legal system, the church, the educational system, the penal system, and the government, to name a few.

When a group of people gets too proud and takes righteous matters into their own hands, they are usually motivated by their hatred towards those who don't believe in their values or their causes. This hatred gives way to a new form of justice; violence against non-believers.

Before we were attacked on our soil, by international terrorists, we were attacked by domestic terrorists. In the early seventies, small factions of anti-government groups started springing up around the country, declaring that people should be self-governed, and therefore free to live according to their own beliefs. Predominant among their complaints were mandatory tax payments, gun control, immigration and miscegenation. The power of the governed people transformed into the power of individuals with a common cause.

American terrorists against the American government became a new type of war for the country to fight. Soon we were hearing about the

Posse Comitatus, the Branch Davidians, the New Patriots and Timothy McVeigh. The forerunner and model for these hate groups was the Ku Klux Klan.

Racism is ingrained in every system in the United States of America. Our country was built on the backs of slaves and our government was created by wealthy white men, who owned slaves. "All men are created equal" was a truth under God, but it was not addressed in the laws of the land. Many amendments to the constitution have addressed these problems, yet it still persists.

People of color have learned their own survival skills against these systems to their own advantage and detriment. Codes have become ethnic laws. They have learned how to play the system, in order to even out the score. Yet, in doing so, they end up imprisoned, charged for petty crimes and misdemeanors so they get caught up, tripped up and tied up in repeat offenses. Once they get a record, they are headed on the downward spiral to nowhere.

Doing right becomes a matter of taking their place as the quiet victims in the work place, hoping to be noticed and advanced by their work ethics. Heaven help the Black American male who tries to be assertive in the work place!!!

Governments need to govern with tolerance, peace and concern for individual freedoms, within the constraints of the law. Sometimes governments become large hate groups. It is then, when global governances must take action. We are not as free as we want to be, and for good cause. Governance should bring order and should direct behavior. Total freedom would be chaos.

True freedom lies within the individual. The paradox is that it takes true inner freedom to understand the necessity of governance, and true government to understand the biases ingrained in our system that perpetrate the loss of individual freedom, for certain citizens.

Tolerance is like oxygen.

Pride is like helium.

Pride puffs up a soul until it rises above the air around it. All religions of the world warn against pride. Pride is human, not spiritual. Once you bind yourself to pride, you are required to keep your own balloon afloat and that requires energy. The most powerful human energy is hatred. The most powerful spiritual energy is love.

Choose to lose, or choose to win, or maybe just choose to play, like Patrick James Cutter, or Cutty, as you will know him, a strong, black American male just trying to make it day to day in the USA.

x

Cutty

Patrick James Cutter was born in the small town of Wells, Texas on Christmas Eve 1960. His mother, Ellie was 16 years old when she went through her first childbirth as her older sisters stood by. A full moon loomed over the weeping willows that night, as he was pulled from between his momma's legs and placed on warm linens. He was a beautiful brown baby boy, with broad cheekbones and slits, for eyes. Instead of breaking out into a gusty birth howl, he looked up at his aunties, and his momma, and he smiled.

Forty years later, when I met him, he was still smiling at pretty women.

Soon after his birth, Ellie Cutter packed up her things and her three-month-old son, and moved to Diboll, Texas. Ellie's mother, Laverne, had taken to whipping Ellie with a switch, and calling her a whore and Patrick a bastard. Laverne was an alcoholic. Ellie could have easily wrestled her momma down. She had been wrestling with her brothers for years, but out of respect for her mother and the rest of the family, she removed herself from the unhealthy environment. Patrick's 18 year old father had already run out of town with an older woman.

Ellie took a job at the Diboll town diner and the owners gave her a sleeping room in the back of the store for her and her son. Ellie matured and Patrick grew into a precocious one year old. On December 20, 1961, a handsome young military man, home for the holidays, came to taste some of Ellie's sweet pies that were the talk of the town that Christmas. Sonny Preston had a smile that went from ear, to ear, and Ellie fell in love with him and his cheerful disposition.

One week later, between Christmas and New Year's Eve, Ellie Cutter married Sonny Preston. Sonny returned to the service, and Ellie continued working at the diner. When he was discharged from the service, Ellie, Patrick, Sonny and his sisters moved to St. Paul, Minnesota to start a better life up north.

Ellie got a good job at Ford Motor Company but Sonny was not as successful in securing a job. Black men were not taken any more seriously in Minnesota than they were in Texas, which came as a big disappointment to Sonny. As his family grew, with the birth of one daughter and two sons, his patience failed and he started drinking and fighting with Ellie. Before long he ran off and left them all, feeling like a failure and a burden. Two months later he was found dead in an alley.

Patrick grew up with three substitute fathers. He learned discipline at home, but he also learned life on the street. He graduated from high school and eventually enlisted in the U.S. Marines.

Cutty, as he was known, was 23 years old when he was dishonorably discharged from the U.S. Marine Corps for striking a superior on the head with a bowling pin. Cutty's version was that the superior was drunk, called him a nigger and chased after him with a knife. Cutty had just won the bowling pin in a league championship game and was walking back to the barracks when he was attacked.

The superior's version was that Patrick James Cutter was a crazy man and a danger to the armed forces. Cutty was declared legally insane and court-martialed. He still carries the papers with him, in a black leather bag that holds the contents of his life, in pictures and documents. It is as if holding onto this bag, holds his life together.

Cutty arrived home on a greyhound bus in the summer of 1984. His momma lived in a two-story bungalow in St. Paul, Minnesota where she had raised her four children and her three husbands. Her husbands had long since been kicked to the curb after they had refused to straighten up and fly right. One had been unfortunate enough to take a bullet in his arm on his way out the door, a gentle reminder from Ellie that no man hits a woman in her house.

"I didn't raise my kids to be pimps, prostitutes or drug dealers." This was Ellie's family mantra which was repeated enough to make it a joke among the kids. In the summer of 1984, the St. Paul streets were full of pimps, prostitutes and drug dealers, but Cutty had never paid any attention to them until now.

He started hanging out in a little place called Sugar's Bar, on Oxford and University, with his home boys and his brother, Bo. Cutty and Bo were well known for their fighting skills. Nobody in the neighborhood would mess with the family. Patrick was a lover with a heart of gold, but Bo had a nasty temper. They both had hands that could easily kill a man. Patrick used his wisely. Bo took risks.

Ellie's youngest child, Vernon, who was referred to by his older sister, Johnnie, as "vermin", was only 5'7", but could survive with his quick small frame. He would move in quickly, throw a rock hard punch, and get out the way just as fast. Vernon was a genius with an IQ of 161. Fast, sharp and focused, he sprinted through life, annoying all kinds of people along the way. He could pick a pocket faster than the Artful Dodger, and his older brothers frequently put him to work for them when they needed some fast change. Their big hands were not conducive to his specialty.

Johnnie was tall, strong and beautiful. She was a gentle girl with soft brown eyes and petulant blackberry lips. Patrick, Bo and Vernon made her business, their business, and the poor girl couldn't get close to a boy without her brothers beating him soundly. They would call it "insurance" against him making an unnecessary advance, later on. Somehow, however, she did get close, because she got pregnant in her senior year of high school and moved out of the house. Ellie was almost relieved to see Johnnie go, to relieve the tension of the angry words between Johnnie and her brothers.

Ellie did not approve of any kind of hitting in the house. Hitting constituted an automatic whooping, cursing constituted an automatic mouth wash, and sassing back was never done more than once to Ellie by any one of her four children.

Ellie was the most respected woman in her neighborhood. Even the dogs respected Ellie and would move to the edge of the sidewalk when she was out for her daily walk. Ellie kept her eyes on everything. She could do that without even turning her head. She knew every crack dealer, every hustler, every pregnant child, before they even knew they were pregnant. She wore her straw bonnet and her tinted glasses, as she walked along, stopping only to help the elderly with their flower gardens, or offer the mailman a word of cheer from the Lord.

So when Cutty left the house, the afternoon of August 4, 1984, it was no surprise to anyone that Ellie predicted that her son was going to cross the line, that night, cross the line to a place she could not accept and would not tolerate. There would be war between mother and child, and that war would wage for almost 7 years.

Sugar's Bar, the afternoon of August 4, 1984 was rocking when Cutty and Bo arrived about 5:00. Cutty meandered over to the bar, brushing shoulders with the prostitutes that hung out there. Cutty loved the smell of women, and he took a deep breath as he walked through them. By the time he got to the bar, one or two of them had already bought him tequila. He popped the shots, turned around slowly, leaned his back against the bar, and chewed on a toothpick while surveying the crowd.

Bo poked Cutty in the ribs with a straw. "Check out that action" he said, pointing to a young blonde girl across the room. "Miss Muffet say she looking for a new pimp and she lookin' right at you, bro."

Cutty's eyes caught hers and he smiled, seductively. She nodded back, sized him up, grabbed her purse and took off, out the front door shaking her bouncy little white ass behind her. He took off behind her and followed her outside.

"Hey, lady...", he called after her.

She approached him, took off her sunglasses, and he realized he was looking into the face of a 17 year old girl. He broke out into a deep, vibrating chuckle.

"How old is you, girl?" He chided.

"Old enough." She replied.

Cutty opened his eyes and mouth and laughed out loud.

"You think you is fine, don't you darlin'?"

"Yeh, I know I'm fine. And you could be fine, too, with the proper attire."

"What's wrong with what I'm wearing?" Cutty asked.

"What's right about it?" Maggie replied.

"How would you dress me?" Cutty asked.

"Why don't you meet me at my place at 8:00 and I'll show you". Maggie spoke matter of factly.

"Wait, where do you live? What's your name?"

"Maggie Prim. 906 Case St. Upstairs apartment. Don't be late or someone else will be there in your place."

When Cutty arrived at Maggie's house she had four bags on her bed. She had bought Cutty a black silk shirt, purple silk trousers, suspenders and Stacy Adams shoes. Cutty put them on, and the transformation was complete. He admired himself in the mirror and then he turned back to Maggie and the clothes came off as quickly as they had gone on.

Bo

Bo Preston woke up with a mouth that felt like cotton and a head that felt like cold steel. He had been drinking tequila shots until 3:00 a.m. Cutty had left him with the homies, just before 8:00. The boys had snorted some cocaine, right at the bar, with rolled up one hundred dollar bills. Bo had met a girl named Tammy and as he opened his eyes he saw that she was still in the bed, next to him. "Oh, God", he said as he rubbed his eyes. "You gotta go, now!"

"What's the matter, Bo?" She cooed.

"We're at my momma's house." He replied.

Tammy hopped out of bed and put on her clothes. Bo took her down the back stairs and pushed her out the door. Suddenly he clutched her shirt and pulled her back. "Give me a kiss", he ordered, and then "I'll see you at Sugar's tonight."

Bo went to the bathroom and got in the shower. When he got back out, Cutty was sitting in the living room on the couch with his muscular arm stretched out on the back of the couch. He was dressed up in his new attire and he wore a cocky grin on his face.

"Where did you go last night?" Bo questioned.

"I got myself a new job, Bro. I found myself a lady who can make some money for her sugar daddy." Cutty bragged.

"Damn, brother. I found me a lady, too. You think you can talk her into making some money for me?" Bo asked.

"I'll check it out for you. Where is she?"

"I'm meeting her at Sugar's tonight. I'll introduce you, and you can have a little talk with her." Bo said, excitedly.

"Will do." Cutty answered.

Ellie walked into the room and stopped dead in her tracks. She stared at Patrick in his purple pants and suspenders and the next thing he knew, she had wrestled him to the floor and was holding him in a headlock.

"What the hell do you think you are doing in my house with that pimp garbage on your body." She screamed, breathlessly.

"Momma, stop. Your asthma." Cutty could have easily gotten out of the lock, but didn't dare to upset his mother further.

She released him and looked at him long and hard. Suddenly, out of nowhere, she started

Every Secret Thing

laughing. It turned into uncontrollable hysterical laughter. Pretty soon Bo was laughing, too.

"You sho' look the fool, Patrick". She gasped and laughed even harder than before.

"I won't be looking the fool when I get me a new Cadillac, and a set of gold rings and chains." He said with a smug look.

That got her laughing even harder.

"Oh, my sweet Jesus, son, you'll look the bigger fool than ever. In this day and age, you are going to turn into a '50's stereotype. You more of a fool than I thought."

"Yeah, and I'll be laughing all the way to the bank."

Cutty was embarrassed by the laughter and headed toward the door.

"Don't let me catch you in my house again until you have regained your faculties." Ellie cried after him.

Cutty walked out and slammed the door behind him.

Bo didn't see him again until that evening at Sugar's. Maggie was there, sitting underneath Cutty's arm, and Tammy was sitting at the same table with them, drinking shots of tequila. Cutty still had the same clothes on.

"Hey, bro. Catch up with us." Cutty slammed the bottle down in front of Bo. I'm gonna take your pretty little girl for a walk and a talk." Cutty winked at Bo.

Cutty took Tammy by the hand and started walking down the street.

"Girl, how do you feel about my brother?" He asked, as they walked down University.

"I want to be his girl", she said, quickly.

"Then you need to help him make some money." He replied.

"Yeah?" she replied.

"Have you ever sucked a dick?" he asked.

She blushed. "Why?" she asked Cutty.

"Because you is soooo fine, lady, you could probably make $50 sucking a dick for 10 minutes." Cutty locked eyes with her.

"No way", she responded.

"Oh, yes!!" he replied. "I'll show you".

With that, he set her on the corner of University and Snelling and stood behind her. Within minutes, a white gentleman slowed down. Cutty motioned for him to wind his car around the corner.

"Are you a police officer?" Cutty asked the first question of all pimps.

"No".

Cutty frisked him as he sat in his car, looking at Tammy. Then Cutty opened the passenger door and told Tammy to hop in. "I'll smoke one cigarette, right here on this corner. You stay in the car, pull up to the curb in the next block or two and suck him off. Be back by the time I step on my butt."

Cutty slammed the door and they drove off. Eleven minutes later, they returned. She hopped out of the car and the gentleman returned to the Capitol.

She was ecstatic. "A hundred dollars. He gave me a hundred dollars."

Cutty gave her a high five, took her hand and walked her back to Sugar's.

"Give it to Bo." He ordered.

Tammy handed over the one hundred dollar bill, jumping up and down and laughing. The next thing Cutty knew, Bo stood up and slapped Tammy square on her jaw.

"What the hell, bro? What you think?" Cutty hollered, amazed at Bo's reaction.

Cutty grabbed Tammy by the hand and pulled her behind his back to protect her.

"What you doing, fool? This girl just brought you $100!!"

"She cheated on me." Bo sulked.

"Well what the hell did you expect, fool?"

It took Bo a while to settle down, but Cutty kept Tammy safe behind his back until Bo reached around and took her hand, coaxing her away from Cutty. He then put his arms around her and kissed her soundly on the lips.

"There you go, Bro. You tell her to save the best for last, and you forget about the rest of them. Just save the best, for last. That's you, bro. The best."

With that, Patrick and Bo were in action with Maggie and Tammy. It had become the practice to pimp one girl at a time, that way you couldn't get charged with solicitation. They worked the streets 24 hours a day, pimping, prostituting, selling cocaine, crack and marijuana. Any hustle was fair game, and any adult was play material. The code was never to hurt a child. And then one day, Maggie broke the code.

Cynthia Marlee Preston

Maggie

Maggie Prim. Sexually abused by her mother's boyfriend when she was 13 years old. Ran away from home when she was 15. Started prostituting herself when she was 15. Independent, willful, tough and jaded, she surrounded herself with four girlfriends and a pimp. The pimps were expendable, but the girlfriends were not.

Maggie was attracted to Cutty, right away. He had the right stuff, she believed, to protect her from other men and to love her exclusively. She was an attractive, free-spirited white girl, and he was a big, strong, good-looking African-American man. It was just the kind of match that she wanted.

The rules to their game were that Maggie would always use a condom with a trick, but never use one with Cutty. That way, Cutty felt that he was screwing his woman, exclusively.

When Maggie told Cutty that she was pregnant, in October of 1984, Cutty was thrilled. When baby Tasha was born, Cutty became the sweetest daddy that ever walked the streets of St. Paul. She was his pride and joy. He would buckle her into the car carrier and cruise, stopping all the hoes along the sidewalks to come see his baby.

Cutty ran the household while Maggie ran the streets. Cutty had learned how to turn cocaine into crack, and was cooking it up in his kitchen one day when Tammy burst in and told him that Maggie had been arrested. When Cutty went down to bail her out of jail, he noticed, for the first time, how raggedy she was looking. As they were driving home, he pulled over and pulled up her sweater sleeve. Track lines.

"What the hell are you mainlining for, Maggie?" He asked.

"To get high." She responded.

"That's no way to get high, Maggie. You'll kill yourself and our baby, too." Cutty patted Maggie's swollen belly.

I don't feel so good, Patrick." She replied.

He didn't expect that Maggie was in labor, on that drive home, but her water broke as they walked up the back porch steps. Two hours later, Patrick James Jr. was born, two months premature and very blue. Patrick Junior stayed in an incubator for four weeks until he was strong enough to make it on his own.

When he came home, Cutty and Maggie found that two children were much more expensive and difficult than one. They found themselves leaving the children with Cutty's sister, Johnnie, while they worked the streets.

Cutty worked mostly by night, while Maggie worked by day. Cutty's pager was his key to the streets. He would get a page from the girls after they had finished their work on the street and were all congregating in a hot tub somewhere in St. Paul. Cutty would roll over in his Caddy, bringing the crack with him and they would spend hours buying and smoking his crack while entertaining him and each other. He knew what he was doing, catching them with fresh money and feeding them his fresh crack. Cutty enjoyed watching the girls play with each other in the tub.

Most prostitutes are interested in getting high on sexual feelings, irregardless of the sex of their partner. Men do serve a purpose, however. It's a fairly simple rule, and logical, too. Women want to be filled up. Men want to fill them up.

So Maggie was filled up for the third time with Cutty's baby. This time, Maggie was in terrible shape and the baby girl barely lived. Nicolle was a sweet, quiet little girl. By this time, Cutty and Maggie had a small house and two dressed up Cadillacs. But Maggie was getting out of control on crack, very restless and extremely reckless.

When Nicole was one, Maggie went down to a very sleazy hotel just off of University to meet a trick. When she arrived, she was met by three thugs. They beat her up, raped her repeatedly, slashed her with a knife, and ran over her pelvis with their car. They left her for dead. Unbelievably, Maggie survived but spent three months in intensive care. More surprising than her survival, was the fact that she was three months pregnant with baby Stephen at the time, and he survived, as well.

Cutty took care of the children while Ellie nursed Maggie back to health. By this time Maggie was strung out on all kinds of painkillers. But she healed and gave birth to Stephen on May 9, 1991.

Stephen was the spitting image of Cutty. Cutty gave himself over to his son and decided to make some changes in his life. As he nurtured the infant, Maggie grew worse and went right back into the streets as though nothing had ever happened to her. It was tragic. Even Cutty now knew that there was something wrong with Maggie that he would never be able to undo. After four children, unbelievably, perfect children, Maggie could not control her obsession to prostitution.

On September 11, 1991, Maggie was called by one of her favorite tricks at 8:00 a.m. Cutty had been up all night and was sleeping soundly. But Maggie left, anyway, laying four month old Stephen in the bed next to him. When she returned, she found her son dead and blue, lying peacefully next to his sleeping father.

Maggie called the police and then took off and hid at a friend's house. Cutty was in shock, disbelief and horror. Cutty was arrested for the murder of his son. He was taken away in handcuffs and the other three children were taken into child protection. Once the death was ruled a SIDS death, he was let go to return to his nightmare: all of his children gone, one dead, and Maggie missing.

Cutty did not return to the life he had been living. It felt so filthy and so empty. He admitted himself to a rehabilitation center where he let the last of the crack/cocaine clear out of his system.

Cutty never went back to Maggie. Instead, he got himself a studio apartment in Minneapolis, a job at a full service car wash in the suburbs, and for ten years worked hard and long hours as manager.

It was there that I met him. My 15 year-old daughter, Shea, was hired by Cutty, to wash cars after school, and I had to fill out some papers to allow her to work. I had an instant attraction to him. It was the tender and naïve undercurrent of this very obvious player that possessed me.

I started giving him rides home from work. He started telling me stories of the street. One

Every Secret Thing

evening as I dropped him at his door, he leaned over, took my head in his hands and kissed me with the softest lips that I had ever felt. Then he opened the car door and hopped out and walked into the house without even turning his head to look back.

Six months later he moved in with me in a big, grand older home in Minneapolis. Things were going well for each of us. I was a college professor of English. Cutty took great pride in his work. We found in each other the wisdom of life through experience.

Disaster struck Cutty again January 6, 2001. Cutty's brother, Bo, was shot and killed in the streets of Minneapolis. Cutty could not control his obsession to go back into the streets, late into the night. He wanted to find the man who shot his brother.

Cutty had encountered a lot of racial bias at his job, but he never expected to be fired, by his white suburban boss, for missing work on the day of Bo's funeral. Of course it was an excuse to weed him out because customers were uncomfortable with a black man working inside their car and one had complained that the car wash reminded him of the ghetto.

Some say, "three strikes, you're out", and Cutty had now had his three strikes. Screwed over by the system three times, and mourning the death of a loved one, for the second time, one hoped that he would be able to recover again, but with Cutty, one never knew anything, fo sho.

Terry

Experience that changes us is the fodder of fiction. Our birth day is undoubtedly the day of our greatest struggle and our death day, the day of our greatest sacrifice; struggle and sacrifice, themes of our life between birth and death. Mixed in are joy, sorrow, faith, despair, love, hatred, and desire.

My name is Terry Onstad. I am 46 years old, and have been divorced for 4 years after a 20 year marriage to Randall Onstad. Randall used to say he was a self-made man. Yes, I believed that, but in another sense than he. He had made himself into such an image that I could never find his true personality or character.

After a very unsatisfying marriage, on my part, I had an affair, the only indiscretion to which I had ever succumbed in our twenty years of marriage. To make matters worse, I got pregnant at the age of 41 by my 27 year old black lover, Dante. Randall and I had a fifteen-year-old daughter, Stacy and a ten year old daughter, Shea, at the time.

Randall went absolutely crazy. I was in a state of shock. I wanted the baby so bad, but I knew it was going to be a bad choice. I moved out of my house and Stacy came with me.

Cynthia Marlee Preston

Shea was convinced by Randall that I was a bad person and he forced her to stay at the house. We were only a mile away. We lived together, Dante, Stacy, baby Mia and me, for three years. During that time period, another baby was conceived and born, my first son, Michael. I was 44 at the time of his birth.

Teenagers are strange creatures. Suddenly Stacy wanted nothing more to do with me. She was 18 and went home to her dad. Now Shea wanted nothing more to do with her dad, and came to live with me at the age of 13. This was good and bad. Randall had done a number on her head, trying to convince her that I didn't love her anymore, and that the new babies were my replacements for Stacy and Shea. Stacy was old enough to know better, but Shea was only 13 and had been hearing this for the past three years.

Shea started hanging out with a rough group of kids and getting into trouble. Pretty soon, she got me evicted from my apartment, Dante left me and moved back to his mother's house in Illinois, and Shea, Mia, Michael and I moved into the inner city, far away from my past, and on the brink of my future.

When Shea went looking for a job, I met a man who intrigued me, her boss, Patrick Cutter. We would give him rides home, after work, because his driver's license had been suspended for speeding. He would tell us crazy stories about street life. He would give Mia treats and make Michael laugh. He made us all laugh. God smiled on me the day he put Cutty into my life. Sometimes I wonder if he is just a dream to add some excitement to my life and to help me heal from my broken heart. With a man like Cutty, one never knows anything, fo sho…

Cynthia Marlee Preston

Bo

Bo Preston was walking on Franklin Ave at 11:30 pm on January 6, 2001. He was looking for crack and he knew that DJ Evans was selling. The years had not been kind to Bo. His skin looked thick and ashy, his hair had smatterings of gray, he had cuts and bruises on his face and deep sockets around his eyes, but he was wearing fine clothes and jewelry.

Bo had just come into a little money through a deal he was working on. He hadn't told anyone about it because if anything leaked, he might lose on a very lucrative opportunity. But this night, he felt like life was going to be taking a turn for the better.

As he walked along, he heard a car pull up behind him and stop. Someone got out of the car but did not turn off the motor. He looked back and saw a hooded figure coming toward him with a gun. Bo turned around and ran toward DJ's steps, but just as he got in the yard, he felt a hot flash in the back of his head. He continued up the steps, tripped and that is the last breath he drew in his lifetime.

It was a strange sensation to die, like life was moving into slow motion. He never saw his killer. Instead, he saw his brother's face as his life faded away. "Cutty", he called, "Cutty, help me." But

Cutty was far from Franklin, that night, Cutty was not there to take Bo's back.

Cynthia Marlee Preston

Chapter 1

Wednesday, January 24, 2001
8:00 a.m.

The sun was breaking up into prisms of color on my wall when I awoke. The doorbell was ringing. I rolled over and looked to the other side of the bed. Cutty was gone but I could still smell his Irish Spring and Coco-butter scent in the sheets and pillows. I squeezed my fists, my hands were numb and my fingers tingled. I wrapped my maroon velvet robe around me and went to the door. It was the Minneapolis police, two officers. I opened the door. They stood there, their suits as pressed and crisp as their voices. They handed me a white sheet of paper.

"Are you Terry Onstad?" the taller, black officer asked.

"Yes", I answered with a quiver in my voice as I got an instant lump in my throat.

"We have a warrant to search your home." The shorter, fatter, red-looking officer said, in a brusque tone and with an attitude of superiority.

"Why? Search for what?" I questioned.

"Evidence in a murder case." He replied.

Cynthia Marlee Preston

My heart skipped several beats and then started racing. I felt like I was going to faint and my hands got shaky.

"Murder? Is this about Bo Preston's murder?"

"No, ma'am. This is regarding a murder that occurred last night".

My thoughts were racing. "Oh, my God. Is Cutty dead? Or, did Cutty kill someone, while looking for Bo's murderer?"

"Who was killed?" I asked, my mouth shaking.

"Ma'am, did Patrick James Cutter stay here last night?" The red-faced, short, apple-looking officer asked me with his stern demeanor.

"Yes." I responded.

Was he here between 12:00 midnight and 1:00 last night?"

"Yes!" I lied.

Cutty had been out every night since Bo was killed on January 6, 2001. He hoped to find clues to the murder of his brother. The police had not been rigorous about this investigation, and it was starting to anger Cutty. They had interviewed Bo's wife, Tammy, and she had told them that Bo had picked her up in what she suspected was a

Every Secret Thing

stolen car, just hours before he was murdered. She had a full description of the car, yet the interviewing officer wasn't taking any notes.

The officer stared me in the eyes for what seemed like 20 minutes, but was, I'm sure, only a few seconds. He then pushed past me, knocking my shoulder as he walked towards the kitchen and Shea's bedroom, in the back of the house.

"My daughter is sleeping back there, sir." I called.

"Why isn't your daughter in school?" He came around the corner and glared at me.

"I home school my daughter." I replied.

I got the same scoff from him that I got from nearly everyone who heard that I was home schooling, Shea. It irritated me, the simple minds scorning everything but structured education, which I believed had failed my daughter.

"I'm a professor of English at the U., sir. I have a right to educate my own child."

"Your daughter has a police record, ma'am. She is a suspect in this murder investigation, as is your, 'whatever', lover, friend, beau, but I'll just call him a THUG, 'cause his record is as long as my arm, and I don't like what I'm seeing here!!!"

I felt the fear of intrusion come over my family. All my freedom seemed to be overshadowed with fear. I turned to the taller officer.

"Who is dead and what are you looking for in my house?" I asserted myself for the first time.

"Ma'am, if you don't mind, I think you should take the young children into another room while we talk." He replied, softly.

I hadn't noticed that Mia, 3, and Michael, 2, were standing behind me.

"Mia, be momma's big helper and play with Michael in the bedroom for a while." I replied as quietly and calmly as I could.

Mia took Michael by the hand and walked him back to the bedroom.

"You have some very well-mannered children, Mrs. Onstad." The officer was genuinely impressed.

"Thank you."

"Yes, I am aware of the death of Bo Preston, ma'am, ...may I call you Terry?" The tall officer was talking to me, while the short fat one messed up my home.

"Yes, please do." I replied.

Every Secret Thing

"O.K., Terry. Bo Preston was killed on Franklin, on the steps of an apartment building. He didn't live in that apartment, and we are doing our best to find his murderer. Last night we found another man murdered a few blocks from where Bo's murder occurred. He was an African American male, about 31. He didn't have any identification on him, but he was very well dressed. We got a phone tip, by a young woman who wouldn't identify herself, at about 7:00 a.m. She told us to talk to you, Terry."

"I was home last night, all night. I didn't murder anybody. Nothing happened!!" I panicked.

"We aren't saying that you did, Terry. This is standard procedure for all murder investigations. Please sit down and remain calm. I am going to show you a picture of the victim." He looked at me with concern.

"This is not going to be pleasant, even if you don't know this man. But, if you do, I need you to identify his body."

The tall officer pulled out a picture and placed it on my lap. Like a bad dream, I looked down into the face of Dante Dean Johnson's dead body, lying on the street. There was only a little blood in a hole in the center of his forehead. His eyes were open. His mouth was opened. Mia looked so much like her daddy that I was suddenly sick to my stomach, looking at the picture of my cold, dead, babies' daddy. I stood up, holding my stomach.

"That's Dante. That's my babies' father. I was with him for four years. That's my Dante." I said.

"Sit down, Terry. You are as pale as a ghost."

"I can't sit down. I can't even believe what you are showing me. Who would kill Dante? Why?"

"Someone wanted him dead. We don't know why, but it looks like it might be a mob hit. Do you know anything about Dante's involvement with the mob?"

Just then Cutty pushed open the front door and walked in with a newspaper. I tried to run to him but I felt like I was running in a tunnel. I was trembling. Nausea continued to rise up in my stomach. I fell forward and saw the piano about the same time it knocked into my face and head. I remember nothing more from that day.

Chapter 2

**Thursday, January 25, 2001
2:30 a.m.**

When I awoke, I was in a hospital bed. I felt confused and my head was throbbing. In spite of feeling dizzy, I sat up and swung my legs to the side of the bed. I dropped to the floor. My legs were weak, but I took a few steps and felt stronger. I remembered the officers being at my house and my fear that Cutty was somehow involved in a murder; but, when the officer showed me the picture of Dante, my head was reeling in shock and confusion.

Dante was still living in Illinois with his parents. He had come around and called a few times, but he was rarely in the Twin Cities, as far as I knew, and when he was here, he would call and visit the kids. This image of him walking on Franklin Avenue at midnight and being shot in the head by a mobster didn't fit into anything that I knew about him. However, Dante was very secretive and his private life had become off limits to me, since Cutty had moved in with me.

My brain felt raw. Tears welled up in my eyes as I remembered Dante and me at our best. He was my best friend for a long time. He would look at me with his big brown eyes and give me his crooked smile and I loved him very much. Mia is a miniature Dante, right down to the crooked smile. It is really remarkable.

Mia and Michael would never see their father, again. My heart ached for them. My soul was stretched by the burden of his death. My mind felt injured, like just thinking about him, hurt as sharply as a physical wound. I could feel depression engulfing me, so I tried to put the sadness on hold and think of the facts. Dante was a straight arrow. He didn't drink, didn't smoke, and went to bed early. He ate right and exercised, regularly. I really didn't understand how or why he would be in town, out on the street and killed by a bullet.

I didn't like the fact that they were asking me questions about Cutty's whereabouts on that night. Cutty had no interest in Dante. Cutty was not a jealous man. The two had met, one time, before Cutty moved in with me. Dante had come to town unexpectedly to visit me at our new Minneapolis house, and Cutty arrived at my door at about 10:00 p.m. Cutty came in and I introduced him to Dante. They shook hands.

"You have some beautiful children, man." Cutty said to Dante.

"Thank you." Dante looked up at Cutty.

I made some excuses to Cutty, asking him to leave before Dante got mad, and he slipped out the front door quietly and calmly.

Dante watched Cutty's back, all the way out the door, and then looked at me with disgust and shook his head back and forth.

"You let THAT, into your house?" Dante asked.

"He's a nice man, Dante." I responded.

"He's a THUG, Terry. I don't want him around my kids."

"Well, you don't have any choice in the matter, Dante. You left me, remember?"

"You need to come to Illinois to live with me. You'll get yourself into all kinds of trouble here." Dante told me.

That was the last time I had seen Dante, although we had talked to each other on the phone, a few times. He had eased off on Cutty, and had just taken a disinterested approach to everything in my life.

I knew one thing, for sure. I didn't want to be questioned by police until I knew what had gone on since I passed out yesterday morning. I could tell that they had sedated me, as I had to wiggle my hands and toes to get feeling in them.

I walked to the hospital room door and opened it, softly. There was an officer posted outside my door. His eyes were closed. I slipped through, suddenly remembering my IV. I ripped the tape from my arm and pulled out the needle. I felt no pain. I started trembling as I ran on my bare feet down the hall and found a stairwell. With a full rush of adrenaline, I ran down eight flights of stairs to the basement.

The sign on the stairs said "Cafeteria" and I opened the door and looked around. To my left, a red "exit" sign caught my attention and I ran toward it. It took me to a cement laundry room where I grabbed a few towels and a large blue doctor gown. I put the gown over my white, backless gown and felt a small comfort with the extra warmth. I saw the door and I pushed it open into the January air. I ran into the street barefoot and caught the first bus to St. Paul where I got off at Cutty's mother's house.

Ellie took me into her living room and got some warm wet towels for my feet. She brought me a hot cup of cocoa and then sat down on her couch and looked at me.

"What's going on, Ellie?" I asked.

"Patrick has been arrested for murdering your babies' daddy. They found a gun in your bedroom, in your laundry closet."

"A gun?" I asked, astonished.

"That ain't all, child. They took your little ones into protective custody and they took Shea to the juvenile center in Hennepin County."

I couldn't believe what I was hearing. It took a moment to try to make some sense of the new developments.

"Girl, Bo is still warm in the grave and now they have Patrick in jail for murder."

I looked at her strong face, which was now slightly trembling. She looked so sad, and I felt very sad and alone, too.

"Ellie, a gun? In my bedroom closet? I don't have a gun. I hate guns."

Ellie held a Kleenex to her nose and regained her composure.

"They believe that Patrick killed Dante out of jealousy."

"No! No way!"

"Patrick is a jealous man, Terry." Ellie looked deeply into my eyes.

"I have never seen him act jealous. I would say the man does not have a jealous bone in his body!!!" I stated, emphatically.

"I know my son, Terry. What you see with Patrick is not always what you get. Don't let him surprise you. Anyway, it doesn't matter to the police, darlin'. Patrick has a record as long as his arm. They feel justified in holding him for 72 hours."

"I am really confused, Ellie. Why was Dante in town, in the first place? I haven't seen him for months. I can't believe that he would come to town and not call me or visit the kids. That's not like him!"

"You never know 'bout some of these niggers, child. Some gots some strange ways about them."

Ellie's voice sounded very philosophical as she imparted her African-American female wisdom about their men upon me. I was grateful for the simplicity. I was one to always make too much of analyzing the motivation and intent of others.

I sat back in my chair and sipped on the cocoa. I looked around the living room at the

African artifacts, the plants, the bookshelf full of pictures, nameless faces, mostly. Old pictures from a dusty Texas town. New pictures of grandchildren in clean, pressed clothing. A picture of Patrick James Cutter, US Marine. The framed funeral brochure from Bo's funeral, held just three weeks ago. I looked at the ceiling and closed my eyes. My body felt light. White and gray pictures started forming behind my closed eyes.

The first was a picture of Shea. She was at the juvenile detention center. She was no stranger to her surroundings. She had been there many times before. Shea had been struggling since she moved back in with me. At 15 she already had a record of car theft, fleeing the police, open container, driving without a license, and assault. She had calmed down quite a bit in the last six months, since Cutty had moved in with us. He was a wonderful influence on her and she was off probation and had no arrests since he arrived.

The second was a picture of Cutty, his big strong body dressed up in an orange jumpsuit, prison style. He too, was no stranger to his surroundings, but his face was angry, and his eyes were dark. He was not about to let the system get him again. He was an innocent man. He was running his thick, black fingers back and forth across the bars of his cell and his mouth was moving, but I couldn't hear a word he was saying as I slipped into a deep sleep.

Every Secret Thing

Chapter 3

Thursday, January 25, 2001
9:15 a.m. Hennepin County Jail

Patrick Cutter sat in his holding cell on the first floor of the Hennepin County Jail. Down the hall a guard was eating a raspberry Bismarck and drinking a cup of coffee. He was looking at Patrick's file and he dropped a little jelly on one of the pages. It formed a red stain on the page, and he brushed it in with a napkin. Then he wiped his chin and stretched back in his chair.

From down the hall he heard a yell.

"I need a lawyer, I want to see a lawyer this morning. You can only hold me for 72 hours without evidence. I'll sue your mother-fuckin asses if you try to hold me longer. I know the law!!!. I know the law!!!"

"Shut your yapper, Cutter. We can do whatever we like to a cold-blooded murderer." The guard replied.

"Oh, no. I got rights and this country got laws to protect me, even if I am just a fucked-up nigger, to you."

"You got that right." The guard replied.

"You a smart-ass, ain't you. But no one smarter than Big C." Cutty replied.

"Ah, save it for the cunts that you pimp, BIG C!!!" The guard roared in laughter.

"That's cold, man. I have been OUT of the business for 10 years." Cutty roared back. "But this system is unforgiving. Fuckin' unforgiving, especially if you are a black man in America!!!"

"OK, Cutter. You'll either be charged or released within 72 hours, now shut up so I can take five, and I might share a cigarette with you later."

Cutty leaned his forehead up against the bars and ran his thick, black fingers back and forth across the bars of the cell.

Chapter 4

Thursday, January 25, 2001
10:00 a.m., Juvenile Justice Hall, Hennepin County

Shea Onstad walked down the hall to the juvenile detention school. She was a pretty, tall thin girl with white blonde hair and soft green eyes. She had the appearance of being very self-contained and very comfortable with herself.

She held on tight to a notebook. Her feet were shackled. She wore a pair of grey sweatpants that she had hiked up to just below the knees. The detention officer made a motion toward her legs and told her to pull down the sweat bands to her ankles. She gave him a look of contempt and then complied.

"I want to talk to my mom", she said.

In spite of her wild ways, Shea was really just a little girl who had a very generous and tender heart. She loved her mother, whom she felt was her only ally in a world that seemed to favor a different type of girl than Shea.

"You can call her during phone time, this evening." The officer replied.

"I need to talk to her now!" Shea stated emphatically.

"What for?" The officer retorted, getting annoyed with her attitude.

"I want to tell her something."

"What?!?"

"Are you my mother, man?" Shea asked, sarcastically.

"Cut the attitude. What's going on?"

"I killed someone." She said, staring into the officer's blood-shot blue eyes.

He stood there for a moment, not sure what to believe. This pretty teenager with pale, soft skin, like that of a flower petal and sea green eyes, looking at him with such anger and saying that she had killed someone, caught him off-guard.

"You killed someone?"

"Yes, I killed my mom's ex-boyfriend." She replied.

"Are you ready to issue a statement to that effect?"

"Yes, I am". She looked down at her hands with some uncertainty.

"Oh, boy" he sighed, "let's go down to the office, then".

If you looked very carefully, as they walked down the hall toward the office, you could see Shea's blonde head trembling and her fingers fidgeting in anxiety, but her back was straight and tall and she kept pace with the officer in spite of her shackles.

Chapter 5

**Thursday, January 25, 2001
10:30 a.m., Ellie's House**

The sound of a shrill telephone broke my slumber. It took me a moment to figure out where I was. Ellie had covered me in an afghan and I was reclining in her living room chair. I grabbed the phone out of habit.

"Hello" I answered.

"Who's this?"

"Who is this?" I responded.

"Maggie."

"Hi, this is Terry." I said.

"Where's Cutty?" she questioned.

"In jail." I responded.

"So, what's new!! What for this time?"

"False charge." I responded.

"As usual." She came back.

"Maggie, what's up?" I asked, tiring of her sarcasm.

"I didn't get my child support check, yesterday."

"Cutty got fired." I explained.

"Great. How am I supposed to pay my fucking rent?"

"How much is it?" I asked.

"$500."

"I'll write a check." I replied.

"Don't bother. I don't want your goddamn money. Cutty's the one after your money, not me!"

"Whatever, Maggie."

"I make my own way, girl. I may be 33, but I still got it going on." She bragged.

"How are the kids?" I asked.

"Tasha's gone."

Tasha was Cutty and Maggies' 16 year old daughter.

"Where did Tasha go?"

"Hell if I know." She replied. "She probably went to your house. She thinks the sun rises and sets over your head!"

"She's a good girl, Maggie. Your raised her well." I said.

"She hates me." Maggie responded.

"Teenagers hate everyone." I said. "Maggie, I've got big trouble."

"What?" Maggie sounded genuinely concerned.

"My kids' dad, Dante, was murdered the other night."

"Oh, my God. You have to be kidding?"

"I wish I was, but I'm not!! He was murdered. They took Patrick to jail and are holding him. They put Shea in Juvenile Hall and are questioning her. They put Mia and Michael in Foster Care. The cops are looking for me right now. I ran from the hospital last night. There was an officer posted at my door, but he was dozing when I left."

"Why did they go to such extreme measures, so soon?" Maggie questioned.

"Because they found a gun in my house, but it wasn't my gun. I don't have a gun and never would."

"Was it Patrick's gun?" Maggie asked.

"I didn't know Pat had a gun." I answered, surprised by her question.

"His momma keeps one in her bedroom. He's been known to borrow it. Run upstairs and look on the top shelf of her closet. I'll hold on the line."

I got out of my chair and ran upstairs to Ellie's room. I pushed open the door. She must have left for work in a hurry because her bed was unmade. She was not one to leave a bed undone. I opened the closet door and felt along the shelf. I felt something cold and hard. I took the blue, steel gun into my hands. It was a lot heavier than I expected. It felt good to hold onto it, but I put it back and ran back downstairs. I picked up the phone, again.

"It's there. I saw it."

"Good, that means Patrick is clear. That is the only gun he will handle. Says it's unlucky to touch another. Now tell me, what did the officers tell you about the murder. Try to remember everything."

"They said that it looked like a mob hit!" I remembered, suddenly.

"OK, good, Terry. They are playing 'spook the family', right now. They are trying to put pressure on you to remember every little detail about Dante, but they know they got the wrong people locked up. They are looking for ties to the mob. They have two law breakers in your family, Cutty and Shea."

"Maggie, what kind of a mob have we got in Minneapolis?"

"Cubans!! You've never heard about them? They are a bad lot. Rotten to the core. They run all the drug and arms traffic here."

"Really?"

"Yes, really. In fact Patrick got himself messed up with one of their women, once. He called her "Cuba". That's all I know about her, and all I want to know about the mother-fucking bitch. But he had to go to the GD to get himself out of that jam."

"What's the GD?"

"Damn, girl. Gangster's Disciples?? The Blues? A Gang, girl, a powerful gang."

"Maggie, how could you stand to live around all that stuff?"

"It ain't hurting me, girl. I make money off of all of them!! What I wanna know, is how was your babies' daddy messed up with the Cubans?"

"You got me? He was clean, Maggie, very clean, a straight arrow."

"Was he a cop?" Maggie asked.

"No, but his cousin was and his best friend was. In fact, his cousin was Shea's D.A.R.E. teacher in 5th grade. Looks like he failed with Shea."

"Terry, you are like the model citizen, and Shea is a little gangster. Patrick and I are both 'off the hook', and Tasha is a model teenager. Go figure?" Maggie sighed.

"Blame it on El Nina." I sighed, too.

"Girl, stay where you're at and I'll come pick you up in twenty minutes to give you a ride home." Maggie said.

"Yeah, that sounds good, Maggie. Thanks. I'll get ready."

Chapter 6

Thursday, January 25, 2001
11:00 a.m., Hennepin County Jail

"Somebody tell that man to shut up", Officer New shouted at the guard. Patrick Cutter was yelling from his cell again.

"What do you have on me? You better release me before I sue the City of Minneapolis for false arrest."

Officer New walked down the hall and stood in front of the cell.

"We are releasing you. Shea Onstad has signed a confession to the murder of Dante Johnson. Said she did it to protect her mother".

Officer New unlocked the cell and as Patrick Cutter walked past him, the officer whispered "watch your ass, Cutter, 'cause I'll be watching it, too!"

Unimpressed, Cutty walked to the guard and recovered his possessions. As he put on his gold watch, he stood still for a moment and looked at Officer New.

"Shea confessed to the killing?" He asked.

"Yes, this morning. Signed a statement and everything. Closed book."

"You believe that garbage? A young girl trying to take the heat for what she might suspect her mother did?" Cutty sneered.

"I believe what I am told and what I read, Mr. Cutter".

"That makes you a double damn fool, with no disrespect, officer."

And with that, Cutty walked out the door, leaving the officer staring at his back.

Chapter 7

**Thursday, January 28, 2001
10:45 a.m.**

I believe that no matter what the dangers around us, we have a safe place within ourselves where we can rest. Somehow, I had found that place after talking to Maggie. I floated through Ellie's house, looking for clothes to wear. I went upstairs to her closet and found a sweatshirt and pants. She had a nice warm ski jacket in the closet, so I put that on, too. Suddenly, as though I had another body inside me, moving my arms, I reached up into her closet and took the gun down. I turned it around in my hands for a while and then put it inside the inner pocket of my jacket. I floated back downstairs, still feeling the warmth within that told me to follow my destiny in this situation and that all would come out fine.

I didn't want to do it, but I had to call Randall, Shea's father, to tell him what had happened. I sat down on the couch and dialed his number at work.

"Randall?"

"Yes."

"I've got some bad news."

"What now?"

"Dante was murdered the other night."

"That's bad news? One less nigger in the world?"

"Randall, Shea is being held in Juvenile Detention for questioning."

"What?"

"They found a gun in my house."

There was a long pause, longer than I had expected, and then a calm voice, which surprised me further.

"So, they found a gun in your house and suspect Shea? Why wouldn't they suspect your gang banging boyfriend?"

"He is being held, too."

"And you, Terry? You should be a suspect before Shea."

"I don't have a record, Randall."

"You fucking got a record with me, bitch. You fucked up, bitch!!! How could you let this happen. YOU WILL NEVER see Shea, again. I'll have my lawyer on this so fast, your…"

I hung up the phone. I didn't need it. Just then I heard a horn honking, impatiently. Maggie was here. I ran out to the car. She drove a 1986 Monte Carlo, metallic royal blue with a black vinyl roof and 20 inch gold spoke rims. I opened the door and hopped into the plush leather seat and set my wet, slushy boots on the one inch thick blue carpet.

"Nice car, Maggie."

"She's my baby."

Maggie pulled away from the curb and peeled out. I grabbed the armrest and braced my legs. Shit, she drove just like Cutty.

"I'll take you home. I want to see if Tasha's there, anyway, but first, I need to make a stop at a friend's house."

Maggie held out a half-full bottle of Jose Cuervo Gold tequila.

"Want some?"

Damn, I hadn't had liquor in the car since high school. But for some misbegotten reason, I took the bottle.

"Got salt and a lime?" I joked.

"In the glove box." She answered.

I opened it up, got the salt, licked my fist to wet it and poured the salt across my fist. Then I numbed my tongue with the salt, drank as much of the tequila as I could and pushed the lime into my mouth, squeezing it under my lips and biting down on it with my teeth. Damn, that was a rush. I felt exhilarated. I turned to Maggie with that big green rind in my mouth and smiled a green smile.

She giggled, and then she burst out laughing. That was the first time that I had ever heard Maggie laugh. I had only met her a couple of times, when she came to pick up Tasha, but she was a pretty hard-core chick. I noticed how cute she was when she was smiling. I could now see the girl that Cutty had fallen in love with.

"Your turn." I coaxed.

She licked her hand, I salted it, and then she took that bottle and killed it. I felt pretty light-headed by then and I started laughing as I passed her the lime from the glove box. She squeezed all the juice out of that lime, chewed up the rind and swallowed it. This time I cracked up. She turned to me.

"You wanna get some more?"

"I'm down wit' you, sista.'" I replied.

She cracked up, again. We pulled into Chicago-Lake Liquor and she sent me in to get it. I bought a fifth of Jose Cuervo Gold, a pack of Newports and went back to the car. When I got in, she was lighting a blunt. I knew what it was, but I was not a smoker. She hit it three times and passed it. Even though I hadn't smoked since college days, I hit it three times, too. It tasted good.

"Look", Maggie said as she drove down Lake Street toward Longfellow Ave., "I've got an old friend that I need to see for about 15 minutes. Will you just wait in the car?"

"Sure", I replied, "I will just wait here for you, with Jose." I laughed.

"She bounced across the yard and up to a back door entrance. An elderly man let her in. I wondered if he was a trick. I didn't really understand the world of prostitution.

I could feel the effects of the pot. It warmed up my head and slowed down the clock. I opened the bottle of tequila and took another shot. Suddenly, all my cares and worries evaporated. I knew the police would be looking for me, but I felt safe in Maggie's plush warm car, listening to some rap...

> "I'm driving down the highway,
> Making money the fly way,

> But there's got to be a better way,
> A better way...."

A better way, huh? Isn't there always a better way to live your life? That better way is what drives us to achievement, or drives us crazy.

The sun was shining brightly, making the snow glisten in the light. The naked trees stood tall next to the well-dressed evergreens. I must have been one of the only Minnesotans that would admit that I loved winter. I could accept hardship, even embrace it. I imagined that most of the people in the U.S. feared hardship. Randall was driven by the fear of poverty and hardship, much to the point of being paranoid.

I didn't like thinking about Randall. His angry outbreaks scared me. Shea had grown to hate Randall for all the lies that he had told her. If he succeeded in getting custody, she would fight him before going to his house.

I picked up the bottle of tequila and this time I guzzled some without the trappings of salt and lime. I gagged, but held it down.

Maggie appeared out of nowhere and hopped into the car. Her eyemakeup was smeared and her hair messed up. I was speaking pretty freely, now.

"So what do you get now for a pound of flesh?"

She waved a hundred dollar bill at me.

"Damn, girl. You MUST be good!"

"No, he just couldn't get it up. Gave me extra for my extra efforts."

"And what would they be?" I asked.

"They would be my secrets. Girl, why are you getting up into my business?"

"Fascination, I guess. Sorry."

"Let me hit that bottle, Terry."

I handed her the bottle and watched her guzzle twice as much as I had taken. No gagging, either.

"So does Patrick ever talk about me?" She asked, out of the blue.

"Sure he does." I told her. I just avoided telling her that he hates the fact that she is still prostituting herself with three teenage children in the house, or the fact that he thinks her 21 year old boyfriend, Darius is using her for everything she's got.

Every Secret Thing

"Don't let Patrick hurt you, Terry. That man doesn't know the meaning of the word, faithful, and he won't marry you. He says "marriage is forever, and I have yet to meet a woman whom I want to live with, forever".

I didn't tell her that Patrick and I were engaged to be married in August. I felt bad for Maggie. I knew she would always love Cutty.

"Hey, girl. Quit being so serious!" I told her. "Pass that bottle back my way."

This time I used the salt and lime. I closed my eyes while sucking on the lime. When I opened them again, I was seeing double. I brought them back into focus.

"Are we almost home?" I asked. "I think I might get sick."

"Just a couple more blocks, Terry. Hold on." She encouraged.

I held my stomach and felt the gun in my breast pocket. Half looped, I pulled the gun out of my pocket and pointed it skyward.

"BANG. Bang." I laughed.

"What the fuck!!! Are you crazy, girl? Gimme that gun. You are nuts, girl." She grabbed the gun out of my hands, and pulled up in front of the house.

I struggled with my purse looking for the house key but found out I didn't need it. The front door was open. Maggie steadied me with one arm, held the gun with the other and we stumbled into the livingroom only to find Cutty and Tasha sitting on the couch.

"Christ, almighty," Cutty roared, "What the hell did you do to her, Maggie?" Cutty hopped up and pulled me away from Maggie.

"She's just drunk. We guzzled a little Jose Cuervo Gold, this morning."

"The homicide detective is coming back in two hours. We need to sober her up." Cutty took me to my bedroom and undressed me. He layed me down and covered me up. Then he walked back to the livingroom.

"What the hell are you doing with Blue?" He asked Maggie.

"Terry took it. I just told her to look and see if it was still there." Maggie defended herself.

"You need to keep away from Terry. She has already got big problems. She doesn't need another one. And you need to take that gun back to momma's house. I'm not touching it."

Maggie started crying.

"Tasha, come on, we're leaving". Maggie said.

"I'm not going with you, mom. I'm staying with dad and Terry."

"Patrick?" Maggie questioned.

"She can stay here for a while. She's worried about Shea."

"Why can't you be nice to me?" Maggie sobbed.

"Because you ain't nice to yourself, lady. You need to get yourself a REAL job and take care of our children, instead of taking care of a 21 year old lover who doesn't work and already has 3 children by another woman. What you think!!!!"

"He treats me good." Maggie came back.

"And how would that be?" Cutty put his hand on his hip and looked like his mother.

Maggie didn't have an answer.

"That's what I thought. Maggie, we have had four children. None of them has been taken care of properly. That is my fault and your fault. I'm trying to change. I want them to have a father that they can be proud of. They need a mother that they can be proud of. Think about it, dear." He walked over and hugged her as she sobbed for several minutes.

"You can do it, lady. You're strong. You'll make it"

"I like Terry." She blubbered.

"So do I, honey." Cutty told her, tenderly.

"I wish I had met her first!" She blubbered again.

Cutty laughed out loud.

"Oh, babe, she does not swing that way." Cutty replied, emphatically.

"But, I'm good Cutty. I'm the best." She replied.

"Yeah, honey. I taught you to be the best at everything you do. Now I'm asking the same of you, but adding one thing: Do Right. Remember Dudley Do-Right? Honey, it matters. In this world, it does matter that you Do-Right."

"I love you, Patrick". Maggie had relaxed some.

Every Secret Thing

"Of course you do. And I love you too, baby. Now show me what you're made of, and go to work for the Man, not on the man."

"I'll think about it." She said, gaining her repose. She gathered herself together, gave Tasha a hug and left the house.

"Dad," Tasha said, "She doesn't get it!!"

"Tash—that is probably my fault. Give your momma a chance."

"I'll try, dad."

"Good girl. Now please do me a favor and make Terry a pot of VERY strong coffee. She is going to need it."

Chapter 8

**Thursday, January 25, 2001
Noon**

While Terry was snoring in the bedroom, and Tasha was doing her homework at the dining room table, Cutty was resting in an easy chair and thinking about his family. Cutty was born in East Texas, to a daddy he never remembered seeing. His father, Josiah James, didn't take much interest in baby Patrick, in fact, he even accused Ellie of sleeping with his brother, John, because he thought Patrick looked more like John, than himself.

Young men are so stupid about young women. A young woman like Ellie was not interested in promiscuous sex with two brothers. She was nurturing her romantic need of the hearts and flowers image of love, with one woman, one man, one love and one couple, through thick or thin, through life and death, through sickness and health; that is, until she woke up one morning and vomited on her bedspread.

More romances are ruined by pregnancy than by any other secret thing. And many secret things within the minds of women contribute to unexplained pregnancies. Cutty had his share of indiscretions, made public by the swelling bellies of young girls. Cutty had been a babe magnet for young lonely girls with father issues. He attracted them like flees and they trapped him like Venus flytraps. When he was caught, there was hell to pay with Maggie, and later on, there was child support to pay for Venus1, Venus2, and Venus3. I had met all the "Venii", if that is the proper plural of the term.

There was one theme to all of his "baby momma" including Maggie; they were blonde, blue-eyed, girls, under the age of 20, when he met them, from unstable homes where their REAL fathers were not present. Furthermore, they all believed that if they played the game right, they could trap him into staying. Neediness and sex were the usual forms of temptation. Neediness was the one that was most effective with Cutty because he thought of them more as dependents, than as ex-lovers and felt responsible for their single parent plight.

"Judge not, lest you be judged", the Bible warns. I have heard more talk-show hosts and hostesses standing up on their soapbox preaching about sex and pregnancy, but the plain truth is, when you have unprotected sex, you may get pregnant and you better be prepared to raise the child that is born or give it to someone who can raise it. Cutty took full responsibility for all of his children and did what he could to spend time with them and support their mothers financially.

Cynthia Marlee Preston

African-American wisdom respects all life born out of wedlock. There is a great pride and affection for children and a loyalty to blood that is as sacred as communion wine. The accomplished parent has taught their children how to clean up the house, finish their homework, groom themselves, speak respectfully to adults, sit still in church, eat everything on their plate, and go to bed when told.

In my Northern European heritage, the accomplished parent turns an eye from the messy room, or excuses all childhood behavior away as 'children will be children'. Expectations in the home run shallow, but expectations in public run deep. My people tend to show their love for their children by pampering them, like pretty pets. They prove to their peers that they have raised their children right, if their children can display athletic, academic or cultural accomplishments in public. They measure their parental worth on the number of trophies, honors or awards that Junior brings home.

Cutty thought about how he should be acting as a substitute father to Bo's children, along with his children and Terry's children; however, he decided that it was just about impossible to care for them all, financially, unless he won the powerball. Cutty felt the weight of Bo's death upon him. He felt like he lost his back, his best friend and supporter, and his blood. Bo had a bad temper, so Cutty would always take his back.

But Cutty wasn't there the night that Bo was shot and killed, and that would be a burden that Cutty would bear to his grave. There was no antidote to the guilt that the survivors feel when a loved one dies before his time.

Cutty opened his eyes and looked at his watch. It was already 12:30 and the homicide detective was due back at 1:00. He came into the bedroom to wake me up. He had to work on me for quite a while before I looked out from my bloodshot eyes into his face.

"Wake up, lady. Time to get up and smell the coffee". He coaxed.

"I'm up, I'm up." I answered feeling violated.

I walked out to the kitchen and drank some coffee. My head was bleary, and my hands were shaky. I felt really fearful about the detective's visit. I was at a loss as to explain anything, but I always worried about being falsely accused. Out of the blue, I realized that the last time I had been semi-conscious, Cutty was in jail.

"Cutty, how did you get out of jail?" My mind started clearing rapidly, like clouds blown across the sky and off to the horizon by a persistent wind.

"I was wondering when you would notice." He answered. Unfortunately, the bad news is that Shea confessed to the murder."

"What??? What did you just say?"

"Shea confessed to the murder. They had her sign a statement." He answered.

"Shea wouldn't kill a ladybug, much less a full-grown man."

"I know that, you know that, and the police know that. They are trying to read the reactions of other family members, but they already told us that they are looking for a ringer in this murder. Mob, they think. Nice clean wound from far off. Specialized gun, I'll bet. The ballistics report on the gun in our house will come out clean. It was a plant, by someone."

"You think it was planted?" I asked.

"Of COURSE I think it was planted. You don't think any of us killed Dante, do you?"

"No." I replied.

"What did I tell you about keeping your doors locked?" Cutty stared at me with his hands on his hips and eyes wide.

"O.K., I am guilty of leaving doors opened, because we have so many people coming and going out of this house." I replied.

"My point, exactly. Terry, I don't know exactly how this thing is put together, but we have two totally different men, killed on Franklin, within three blocks of each other, within three weeks of each other, and both of them connected to us? This is no coincidence, darling. This is NO coincidence."

"I'm listening, Patrick." I begged for more of his street smarts before the officer arrived.

"You need to think like a criminal now, Terry. Whoever killed Bo was not the same person who killed Dante. Bo's gun wound was close and sloppy. Dante's was clean and distant. But, there is some connection between the two murders, and it's probable that the two murderers knew each other. I'd guess that Bo and Dante were messed up in somebody's dirty laundry, whether they knew it or not." Cutty was getting deep in thought.

"I just don't understand what Dante was doing on Franklin Avenue, in the middle of the night, in the middle of winter?" I questioned.

"People aren't always what you would expect them to be, Terry. The hustler learns this firsthand. You've got your lawyers and your bankers and your rich suburban wives coming downtown for a little cocaine, or some crack, or for some sex. They ain't getting what they need at home, so the moon draws them out into the streets of downtown. I've seen it time and again. Remember Mayor Benson? One of my clients!!" Patrick bragged.

"You're kidding".

"No, no, no, no, no. I tell the truth!" Cutty made the sign of the cross on his body and kissed his thumb and forefinger up to God.

"So what do you think that Dante was doing on the street?" I asked.

"What do I think? What do I think?"

"Yes, what do YOU think?" I asked. Cutty always did this when he was buying time to think up his answer.

"I think he was a drug trafficker." Cutty replied, matter of factly.

"You're crazy, Cutty. Dante? He wouldn't even take a drink of alcohol."

"You asked me what I thought. WHAT you thought? The man lives right outside of Chicago, and he shows up dead in Minneapolis, on the street, after living here for a while. He starts to

Every Secret Thing

feel the fear on Monday afternoon. He knows his baby momma is nearby, so he calls her home, talking like he is in Chicago, when he is really in her backyard on a cell phone. But he doesn't get to talk to his baby momma, 'cause Big C answers the phone and they argue. He wants to see the babies and you aren't home. I tell him to call back and talk to you and the next thing I know, he barges into the back door of the house. Of all people, he has your daughter Stacy with him!!! Shea and I tell them to leave. It looks to us like Dante and Stacy are hooked up. They visit the kids for a few moments, then threaten custody of the children and leave as fast as they came. Shea and I didn't want to disturb you with this mess, but honey, I think your oldest daughter was doing the wild thing with her step sister and brother's daddy?"

"Oh, gross." It was the first thought that popped into my mind.

DING - DONG

"Terry, you need to keep your mouth shut, on this. Remember the MOUTH, and keep it shut. Don't be running off, like you do, offering information that he doesn't even ask of you. Keep your answers short and your tongue still."

With that, I walked to my front door and looked out at two men in blue, for the second time in two days. I took a deep breath and opened up the door.

Chapter 9

Thursday, January 25, 2001
1:00 p.m.

I opened up the door to the two officers.

"Terry Onstad" one of them asked?

"Yes", I replied.

"Is your daughter Shea Onstad?"

"Yes"

"We have a confession to a murder by your daughter, the murder of Dante Dean Johnson of Rockford, Illinois."

"She didn't do it, officers. She hasn't had a chance to talk to her father or me. We should have been present during any questioning or confessing."

"We will have to wait for the ballistics report to come out before we can take further action. However, she will be held in the Juvenile Detention Center until that happens." The officer reported.

"When can I see her?" I questioned.

"You can come tomorrow, anytime after noon." He responded.

"I have some questions for you, Mrs. Onstad. First of all, I would like to know when you last saw Dante?"

"I haven't seen Dante since March of 2000. He visited me here, unexpectedly."

"Did you ever suspect Dante of being involved in any illegal trafficking of drugs, guns, etc.?" He asked.

"No." I remembered Cutty's advice and kept it short and to the point.

"Do you know if Dante has another girlfriend or close friend who lives in Minneapolis?"

This time Cutty glared at me from his chair.

"No, I don't know." I answered.

"Do you know why your daughter would want him dead?" He asked quickly.

"No." I answered, very calmly and matter-of-factly.

"You're not helping us, ma'am." He said in a disappointed manner.

"I can't help you when I don't know anything."

"Did your daughter, Shea, ever show signs of aggression towards Dante?"

"No."

"Did she like Dante?"

"Shea doesn't like anyone. She is a teenager, remember."

"Have you ever seen Shea or any of her friends carry a gun?"

"Never". I responded.

"Why would she confess to murder, Ms. Onstad."

"I don't know. You can talk to me more after her father and I have had a chance to visit with her. I will be there tomorrow after 1:00 to visit."

The two officers looked at each other and nodded.

"OK, Mrs. Onstad. We will leave you alone for today. We will have more questions after the ballistics report comes out."

The officers stood up and nodded to me, and then turned to Cutty and nodded.

"Nice to see you again, Mr. Cutter." Officer New said to Cutty.

"My pleasure." Cutty said, civilly and coolly.

Suddenly Cutty stood up turned around, dropped his pants and bent over.

"Keep your eye on the ass, officer." He turned his head around and grinned.

Officer New lunged toward Cutty, while the other officer grabbed Officer New.

"Let it go, Roger. Just let it go."

I was horrified. Why would he do that after things had gone so well. Damn him, sometimes!"

"I apologize for his behavior officer. It's been hard on all of us." I tried to appease.

"Goodbye, Mrs. Onstad".

And with that they opened the front door as a rash of cold air blew in, and slammed it behind them.

Chapter 10

**Thursday, January 25, 2001
6:00 p.m.**

I stood in front of my African-American Literature class as the students marched in from the cold carrying bags full of MacDonald's burgers and fries. They stamped the snow off their Doc Martin boots and were laughing and talking as I welcomed them back from winter break.

"OK, class. Let's get cracking. If we can get through this assignment I will give you all the opportunity to go home early tonight."

"All right, tight. You rule, Mrs. Onstad."

"OK. We are discussing Richard Wright's *Native Son*. I hope that you have all had the opportunity to read through the first few chapters."

"It gives me the creeps." Naomi Johnson stated. "The rat, and the poverty, and the way they talk to each other. I don't like the book, so far."

"That is what is called the 'tone' of the book, Naomi. The tone is dark and foreboding, right from the start. The rat actually plays a role, by foreshadowing the plight of one of the characters. I'm not going to tell you any more about that, but I want you to think about that as you are reading along." I said.

"Julie, will you read the introduction to the book, out loud, for the class. Come on up front."

My mind was not on lessons tonight, so I let the class read out loud bringing up important points, as necessary. I had taught this class so many times it was second nature to me, now. After about two hours, I asked the class "Does anybody want to continue until 10:00?"

"Hell, Na!!!!!"

"See you next week, class dismissed". I left the classroom, relieved.

Chapter 11

Thursday, January 25, 2001
7:00 p.m., Franklin Avenue, Minneapolis

Cutty walked down Franklin Avenue and lit a cigarette. He passed a group of four brothers and stopped next to them.

"What up, man?" one asked.

"What up, boys. Got the chronic?"

"Waiting on it, man. What you want?"

"A dub. But I want to see it first."

"It's green."

"Yeah? What's going down with the hits in this hood, bro? Heard that there was another hit since my brother, Bo, was killed." Cutty asked.

"Nasty, no one know. Cuban's have been hanging around and the po'po hanging low."

"Yeah?"

"This brother that got shot has been hanging around out here since about November. He got a girl wit him, sometime, who is clean. Look like a model right out of a magazine."

"Redbone?" Cutty asked.

"Na, bro, straight up white chick. He live down near Park. That where his homies from, anyway."

"What else do you know about him?" Cutty looked him straight in the eyes.

"I know he sell the powder and the rock. I know he tied to the Cubans, so no one bother him. And I know he got hit by the Cubans, nice and quiet and clean. Nobody talking much about it, Bro".

"OK, man. I'll be back when the crop come in. Later."

Cutty drew the last hit on the cigarette and flicked it into the street. As he walked along he saw something glimmering on the side of the road. It was a pair of sunglasses, very expensive men's gold sunglasses. He looked at them a minute, his big winter coat covering his arms to the finger tips. He picked them up and turned them around in his hands and then he tilted up his head and put them on. He looked at the street light through the dark lenses and thought about the events of the last three weeks. First, his brother was shot and killed on this street just three weeks ago. Drugs? Probably. Theft? Possibly. A drive by, no because someone stopped, got out of the car and chased him up the steps to an apartment building. They found him dead on the front steps. Then Dante was shot and killed a couple of blocks down on Franklin from Bo's murder scene.

"Bang, Bang, You're Dead." Cutty spoke the words out loud and held an invisible smoking gun in his outstretched hand.

Suddenly he thought about the residents of the apartment building where his brother had died. He walked up the steps and looked at the names on the boxes:

> Apt. 1—S. Marlowe
> Apt. 2—Vance Ostby
> Apt. 3—Terrell Cox
> Apt. 4—D.J. Evans

"DJ Evans. DJ Evans." There was an Evans family, well known in the city for their forgery ring. Cutty made a mental note.

"Terrell Cox?"

"Cocks crow."

Cutty rang the bell.

Chapter 12

**Thursday, January 25, 2001
7:30 p.m.**

Terrell Cox answered the door. He was a small, black kid, nervous looking with prancing eyes. Cutty recognized a crack user the moment he saw one. He was barely 20 years old and was already missing a front tooth. Cutty's huge presence dwarfed Terrell Cox.

"Hey, Shorty, got a minute?"

Terrell came outside, shivering a bit and lit a cigarette.

"What up?" He asked.

Cutty's chest went out in a deep sigh.

"You know my brother?" Cutty asked.

"Who your brother, man?"

"Bo Preston."

"No, way, man!!!"

"You sho, Shorty? You wouldn't be lying to the Big C, now, would you?"

"I'm cool wit you, man. I know the name. He died on this apartment stoop. But, I ain't never heard of him before that."

"Ever heard of Evans?"

"DJ Evans?"

"Yeah, DJ."

"Dogg, DJ live in number 4. He cool."

"Do I look like a dog? Don't call me dog, man. I'm not your dog."

"Sorry, man. What are you, a cop?"

"No, I'm not a cop. I am just doing the job for them, while they too busy sitting on their thumbs to get out in the street and look for murderers."

"I hear ya, man. Not, me. I ain't no murderer."

"I can see that, Shorty. Now tell me everything you remember about the night my brother was killed."

"There were cops all over. All the neighbors came out."

"Did Evans come out?"

"DJ was hanging on the sidewalk with his homies. I saw him. I was looking for some crunch. He sometimes front me and I do some errands for him – running bullshit. Never know what I got or who's receiving. Usually drop offs. Quick jobs."

"OK, Cox, now we are getting somewhere." Cutty lit a joint and took three deep hits. He passed it to Cox. "You, Shorty, are going to help me catch the fool who killed my brother."

Cutty looked up at the moon, and then at Cox who was chiefing on the joint like a motherfucker and shivering uncontrollably in the frosty night. Shorty passed it back.

"Keep it, bro. We'll be in touch.", Cutty said kindly. "Now, go into yo house before you catch yo death!!!"

Chapter 13

**Thursday, January 25, 2001
9:00 p.m.**

I was sitting in my living room, drinking a glass of wine when Cutty walked in.

"Hello, pretty lady."

"Pretty lady, my ass. Why did you deliberately moon Officer New? Why do you deliberately mock authority, Cutty? You could have been arrested, and I would have been alone, again. You piss me off, Cutty, when you act like a loose cannon."

"I am a loose cannon, babe. And I didn't get arrested, now did I? I know what I'm doing, Terry. Trust me."

"Trust you? What reason do I have to trust you when you act that way?"

"He's a chump. A crooked cop. I know it and he knows it."

"How do you know it, Cutt?"

"Because he tells me he's watching my ass when he released me. What he got to watch my ass for? For what I might discover, that what!!!"

Cynthia Marlee Preston

I shut up and thought about that one for a minute. He was probably right. What did I know about cops? Absolutely nothing. What did I know about Franklin Ave? Nothing. What did I know about murder and motives? I knew shit. I had to trust Cutty. He was all I had in this mess. This was the outer limits, to me. This was reality to Cutty. I had to choose to trust someone at that moment and I chose to trust someone I loved.

"I'm sorry." I responded, and then the tears started flowing.

Cutty came to me and wrapped his big arms around me. We held each other and rocked for a long time. Then Cutty's head leaned down and kissed me on the mouth. I sucked his bottom lip into my mouth and held onto it while I licked it. I could feel his whiskers on my tongue and taste his sweet brown sugar skin.

He moved his hand down my back and up again. I held on tight and he picked me up and carried me into our bedroom. He took off his sweats and stood over me, while I layed on the bed watching. I love big men, and Cutty was one fine, big man. He was all muscle and man.

As he stood beside the bed, I grabbed his bare butt and started licking his stomach. His dark brown body was under my control now, and I loved it. I licked his chest and circled my tongue around his hard black nipples and then nibbled on them. I squeezed his butt as hard as I could and went down on him. I tilted my head up and looked up at him. He was staring at me and then he brought his huge hands up to my head and rubbed my hair.

Yeah, I had him now. He worked the rhythm and I worked the tongue. Suddenly, he hopped on the bed and took me down. I was warm butter in his hands. Nothing in the world mattered except our skin, our hands, our lips and our hips. His powerful thrusts took on a smooth rhythm, his eyes watching mine, his mouth open and his tongue hanging half out.

"Who takes care of you, baby?" He asked, breathless.

"You do, Patrick"

"Who does you like you need to be done?"

"Only you, babe."

"Show me, bitch!!"

And with that he speeded up until I lost myself, my body arched, and that nerve that connects your head to your toes soared off the charts. The pulse of my soft spot squeezed the juice right out of him and we collapsed together, our bodies sweating, our hearts pounding, his heavy body laying on mine.

As the rush died, there was a softness that turned the event into dark night. He fell asleep first, hugging me tight up against his huge chest and cradling me with his arm. I stayed awake for a while, savoring the pleasant after effects of physical love, but before I knew it I had dropped into a deep and dreamy sleep.

Chapter 14

**Friday, January 26, 2001
8:00 am**

Cutty was reading the newspaper when I walked into the dining room. I put my arms around his neck from behind him and pressed my cheek against his.

"Morning lover", I said.

"Hey, baby, you fell asleep on me last night." He replied.

"What? No way. You were sawing logs when I fell asleep." I joked.

"I could have gone a few more rounds." Cutty teased.

"Oh, Right, old man! You were done and gone".

We kissed and I went to the kitchen to make coffee. Cutty called into the kitchen: "Your horoscope says that you need to pick up your kids today and visit your daughter in jail".

"Oh, yeah? And what does yours say?"

"It says that I got some investigating to do. It says I need to bring some murderers out into the open. It says that one DJ Evans is my first suspect."

I came out of the kitchen with two cups of coffee and sat down at the table with Cutty.

"What are you talking about, Cutty?"

"Last night I paid a visit to the Franklin Apartment where Bo died and I talked to a guy named Terrell Cox. He makes runs for his neighbor there, a DJ Evans, a dealer. DJ was hanging on the sidewalk while the police were investigating the murder scene!"

"So, what does that mean? Wasn't everyone hanging around?" I asked.

"True", Cutty replied, "but the rest of the tenants were looking out from the inside. DJ was grouped up with his homies on the sidewalk, kinda like he was keeping his distance, but also, keeping his eye on the thing."

"So, did you meet Evans?"

"No. I'm gonna work with this Cox character as bait to draw him out." Cutty reached into his pocket and pulled out a pair of gold sunglasses.

"Nice spec's, Cutt." I took them out of his hands and read the frame, "Versage. Expensive, too."

"Found 'em on Franklin last night. I need me a new pair." He put them on and mugged for me.

"You look too damn sexy in those glasses, Cutt."

Cutty laughed.

"I don't know exactly how this thing is put together, but I will find out."

"Cutty, don't get yourself killed, too!!!"

"Oh, no. I'm too smart for that, baby. I'm the Big C. Big C ain't going down. Don't worry, now." He reached out and touched my arm, but it offered me little relief.

Chapter 15

Friday, January 26, 2001
1:00 p.m., Hennepin County Juvenile Justice Center

I walked into the center where Shea was being held and signed in as a visitor. I took all of my belongings and put them into a locker and then went over to ring the buzzer for the guard.

"Who are you here to see?"

"Shea Onstad"

"What is your relation?"

"I'm her mother."

"May I see your ID?"

"I just locked it in my locker".

"No visit without a MN Driver's License or State ID card."

I took fifty cents out of my pocket and went back to the locker. As I was getting my driver's license out of my purse, Shea's father, Randall, walked in.

"Damn", I said, under my breath.

"Good to see you too, Terry." He replied in his business-like voice.

"We might as well go in together."

Randall and I walked back to the guard who led us into a small visiting room. After 10 minutes of total silence, Shea was escorted into the room by a guard.

"Baby." I cried.

Her face was swollen up red from crying. I gave her a big hug and held her for a long time.

"Mom, I'm scared."

"I've got my lawyer on it, Shea." Randall chimed in.

"Fuck your lawyers, dad. Why did you even bother to come?"

"Watch your mouth, girl! You're in big trouble here, thanks to your mother and her criminal associates. You need legal representation…"

"Dad", Shea cut him off, "I want to talk to mom, alone".

"Randall, give us some privacy, please, just a few minutes."

Red-faced, Randall walked across the waiting room and looked out a window, his arms folded in front of him, his neck and forehead veins bulging and throbbing.

"Mom, I didn't really kill Dante."

"I know, honey. Why did you say you did?"

"Because I thought you did it, mom."

"Why would you think that?"

"Because of what Dante told me earlier this week."

"Cutty told me he came by with Stacy. Isn't that a trip?"

"He wanted to see Mia and Michael. He came in and played with them. Then he told me that you were unfit as a mother and he would be taking Mia and Michael away for good. I swore at him and Stacy pushed me aside and told me that she and Dante were going to take the kids to Illinois. Stacy is convinced that you are some kind of an evil woman, and then she convinced Dante. I know it's dad's influence, mom. He is a hater!"

"He's just confused." I offered, remembering my 'talking to kids about divorce' lessons.

"I was going to handle it, mom. I asked Logan and Lee to beat Dante's ass, you remember Logan and Lee, from the carwash, the fighting brothers, but before they got to him, he was found dead. I thought for sure you did it when the police found a gun in your closet. I didn't want you to go to jail, mom. I love you too much, and I'm tougher than you."

I pushed her white blond hair back and held her head between my hands.

"Listen, Shea. I'm not guilty of anything. You are not guilty of anything. We are going to get this matter cleared up and get you out of here. Don't worry, baby."

I hugged her as the guard came in and told us that our ten-minute visit was over. Randall and I left together.

"This is all your fault! Your fault that you had those nigger babies. Your fault that Shea is nothing but a criminal at age 15. Your fault that you can't make rational decisions and you let a gangster nigger live in the same house with my daughter. Not anymore, Terry. You can forget about getting Shea back, after this. She is mine!"

His violent words evaporated above my head as I walked along, trying to make some sense of the events that had come to pass.

Chapter 16

Friday, January 26, 2001
1:00 p.m., Franklin Avenue

Cutty was back on Franklin, rolling in his 1989 Cadillac Sedan de Ville, with the 72 gold-spoke rims, gold package, and Cadillac mud flaps. Snoop Dogg was pounding from the stereo system, and Cutty was sporting his new gold sunglasses. Despite the cold, it was a sunny day and there were several people out on the street. Cutty raised his fist to the music, keeping the beat with his arm and his head. When he came to Park, he turned right and rolled by the apartment he had visited the night before. He looked for Terrell Cox but didn't see him. As he came to the end of the block he saw three Hispanic men gathered on the corner.

"Ola", he shouted to the men and pulled over to park.

They looked at him and ignored him, continuing with their conversation. They were older gentlemen, well-dressed and wrapped up in conversation. Cutty got out of the car and walked over to them.

"I said, Ola" he repeated, "Do any of you know of a DJ Evans?"

Their conversation went quiet. They all turned to Cutty with distrust in their faces.

"What do you want?" the youngest man of the group asked.

"I'm looking for some cocaine, boys. I hear he has the best around."

"Who are you?" This time it was the older one with the question.

"Well, let's see. I am known as Big C, to most."

"Get lost, Big C."

"Where are you boys from?" Cutty asked.

"You want to take a ride with us, Big C?" the older asked him.

"Hell, na," laughed Cutty. "I'm just looking for some product."

"Go away and leave us alone. You were impolite to interrupt us."

"Maybe you can extend a greeting to DJ from Big C. Tell him that I am looking for him, and I won't rest until I find him."

"I don't think that he will care, my friend. You see, DJ Evans is dead." The older man glared into Cutty's gold shades. "Now go away and leave us alone."

Cutty was shaken by the answer. He also knew when it was time to leave. This was definitely the Cuban mafia. He had dealt with them before, several years back. While the faces had changed, the mannerisms and stoicism was the same.

"Thank you, my friends", replied Cutty, "I'm sorry to hear of DJ's passing."

Cutty returned to his car and picked up the cell phone as he was driving away. He tried to contact Terry, but she was not answering.

"Shit", he said out loud. "What next".

Another dead man. Another dead man on Franklin. What was going down? And then, with a quick thought, he turned off the road and headed to St. Paul.

Chapter 17

**Friday, January 26, 2001
3:30 p.m.**

Cutty pulled into his old neighborhood and went to the home of Bo's wife, Tammy. He walked up to the door and rang the bell. Tammy answered after two rings.

"Hey, Cutty, what brings you to the hood?"

"Hey, honey, how you doin'?" He gave Tammy a hug as he came through the door.

Cutty looked around the room and complimented Tammy on her fine home. Actually, it was quite bare but he found a stool to sit on in the dining room.

"Sorry to drop in on you like this, girl, but I been doin' some investigating on Bo's murder and I have to ask you something."

"Shoot, bro."

"Was Bo working the street with any Cubans?"

"Cubans?" she laughed, "Damn if I know a Cuban from a Puerto Rican or a Mexican. Why you askin' that?"

"Just a hunch. Did you ever see him with any well-dressed Hispanic men?"

Tammy was quiet for a while and thinking.

"You know Cutty, Bo went to a New Year's Day Party at some baller's house. He go wit another brother who lived in Minneapolis. Bo say it was going to be a fine occasion and he need to look clean. I 'member it coz I was thinkin' I should go, too, but Bo say it was just for the men. Bullshit, I told him. I ain't never heard of no party just for men. I know'd there be hoes there."

Cutty laughed at Tammy's expression, but he was thinking this thing through as she talked.

"Who was the dude that went with him"?

"Dude was called DJ. Fine looking brother. About 30, I suppose. I only saw him that once, and only for a few minutes. He drove a clean Monte Carlo – black and gold and spankin' new."

"Do you think you would recognize him if I brought you a picture?" Cutty asked.

"I'd probably do better to recognize his ass, Lord, he had a fine ass. But I remember the face, too. Clean head, round face, crooked smile, made him look cute."

"Did Bo tell you anything about the party?"

"Yeah, he tell me all about the fine food, jumbo shrimp, thick, juicy steaks, and all you could drink, for free. Oh, and that they all called him Mr. Preston. He said he was going to do some bin'ness with them".

"What kind of business?"

"I never asked Bo 'bout his bin'ness. Never. I never wanted to know nothin'. You know, Cutty".

"Yeah, I know, the MOUTH".

"Fo sho. I don't know nuthin' and I can't say nuthin."

"I'm trying to teach that one to Terry. She always demands to know everything."

"Ah, she a good woman, Cutty. We all glad to see you wit her."

"OK, then baby. You doing ok? Need any money?" Cutty pressed a hundred dollar bill into her palm and closed her fist.

"Just wanted to see what you knew. You've been a good help, girl. I'll be back with a picture, but it probably won't be the ass." Cutty chuckled. Tammy blushed.

"Now take care of those nieces and nephews of mine. Where are they, anyway?"

"Who the hell knows?"

"OK, girl – bye, bye."

"Bye, Cutty."

Chapter 18

Friday, January 26, 2001
3:00 pm

When I left the juvenile jail, I went over to the Child Welfare Office to inquire about Mia and Michael. I got in a long line where you wait for the next available clerk. In sizing them up, I was hoping for clerk number two, a young black woman who seemed friendly and efficient with her customers. Unfortunately, I got the tall, thin, elderly white woman with the glasses and the face that wouldn't crack a smile.

"Hello. I'm here to inquire about my two children?"

"State you full name, please, no nicknames, no initials, and I hope you don't do that hyphenated surname because that wreaks havoc with my system?"

I felt like I was back in second grade and this was Miss Salter, the sternest teacher in the school.

"My name is Teresa Jo Onstad"

"Social Security Number?"

"787-44-5528"

Cynthia Marlee Preston

"Date of Birth – Year, Month, Date"

"What? Oh, my birthday is November 20, 1954".

"You're not following my directions, Mrs. Onstad, Year, Month, Date".

I know I was blushing and I felt flustered by her demeanor.

"Year, uh, 1954, month, 11, date, 20."

There, I did it. I felt like the star pupil, again. Miss Salter wasn't showing any signs of approval, however.

"Address – Street, Number, City, State, County, and Zip".

Damn, this was getting harder. Let me see…

"Ok, Cedar, 1478, no apartment number, Minneapolis, Hennepin, Minnesota, 55407."

"Out of order, Mrs. Onstad. I said State, County and Zip. You gave me County, State and Zip."

"Damn, does that give me two wrong, or just one wrong. It should only be one wrong because I missed the order of one, but it looks like two wrong, because by missing the correct order, two are out of place."

Miss Salter looked at me from over her glasses top. She did not smile. She did not frown. I started sweating.

"Mrs. Onstad, do you think it is a joke that your children have been put into protective services?"

"No, ma'am".

"Then just answer the questions and quit the wisecracks."

"I apologize, ma'am".

"Mrs. Onstad, your children have been placed in Foster care in Hennepin County. The judge will have to sign the consent to release form, and at that time they will be returned to you. We will contact you by phone. Good day."

"Wait, when will that be?" I groaned.

"Anywhere from two to four working days. Considering that it is a Friday, it probably won't happen until Monday or Tuesday of next week."

I was too tired to argue with her.

"We will be in touch with you, Mrs. Onstad. Thank you. NEXT."

Cynthia Marlee Preston

I walked away feeling disgusted with myself. I was not much of a fighter. Cutty was a fighter. Ellie was a fighter. I was a pushover, a marshmallow. I folded when I should have fought. I learned, too well, as a child, to do as I was told. If a clerk told me that they couldn't do anything about a situation, I'd believe them and I'd alter my plans accordingly. Cutty would make his plan, his priority, and he would fight to see that his plan was enacted, as he desired.

Maybe I'm not as sure as he is about the righteousness of my plan? Maybe I feel like God is instrumental in clerks who enforce the rules, and that he has a purpose for my not getting my children back for the weekend? By obeying protocol, without questioning its validity, I got to my destination, but I'd take a more crooked path to arrive there. I would expend my energy on the longer pathway, while Cutty would expend his energy arguing with the clerk, and then the manager, and finally the judge, who would probably take a few minutes to sign the order, just to get the squeaky wheel out of the office.

I viewed myself as a piece of grass, like it says in the Bible. God was the landscaper. If the landscaper didn't want to cut the grass today, should I tear off my own head to make me shorter? It was like that with me for driving, too. I didn't always take the most direct route, or rush to my destination. This made Cutty crazy, when he was in the car with me. He would tell me how to drive.

"Change lanes", he would shout, when I would get behind a car that was making a left-hand turn.

"Why?"

"Why do you want to sit here and wait?"

"Because I'm not in a hurry, and I like this lane." I would answer.

A few weeks ago, I sideswiped a car because he barked at me to change lanes and I did, on command, without looking over my shoulder. Of course, Cutty blamed me for changing lanes without looking.

"You told me it was clear!!" I yelled.

"NOOO, I TOLD you to change lanes, Lady! You are the one who has to make sure the roadway is clear, before you make a lane change. You are the DRIVER of the vehicle."

"Don't tell me how to drive, anymore. You scare me." I said.

"Don't be afraid. Just listen to me, and then use your head, girl."

Cynthia Marlee Preston

Cutty won all of our arguments simply by being illogical and impossible. Just like with the clerks. He won. I lost. I payed the fine and the insurance company raised my rates.

I try not to drive with Cutty in the car, but riding with him is even worse. He calls himself a "skilled driver"; one who can maneuver in and out of lanes going 70 miles an hour, in town, while listening to his full-blown stereo pump out rap at 110 decibels. I couldn't complain, because he couldn't hear me if I did, and besides, he wouldn't change anything if he could hear me. So, what I usually did, was sit back tight, in my seatbelt, believing that if I died that day, in an auto crash, it would be the will of the Lord. This would give me some comfort until we would arrive at our destination.

I was surprised that he never got pulled over for speeding or reckless driving and endangerment. He does get pulled over, and frequently, but never when he is using his "driving skills". No, he gets pulled over when he is "chillin'". Cruising downtown, nice and moderate, looking at the passersby, smiling and waving at people, yelling at the hookers to "get to work", greeting the pimps and dealers, "how you'all doin'", and that is when the police pull him over.

"What's the problem, officer?" Cutty would ask, calmly.

Every Secret Thing

"Suspicious vehicle", was usually the response. "Get out of the car, sir, we want to have a look inside".

Cutty would then scream racial profiling. Cutty was strip searched once, in the middle of a St. Paul street, in the middle of the day. The officer told him to remove his clothing, and he did, with his bare butt, hanging in the wind. He sued the city for discrimination and probably would have won, but he was not properly notified of the court date, and his non-appearance caused the judge to dismiss the suit.

It makes me feel lucky to be white, and ashamed to be white, at the same time. The privileges extended to white Americans are real. The disadvantages of the minorities are real. I believe in them because I have lived them vicariously through Cutty, and through Dante. And, now I have two mixed-blood children who I need to fight for, even though their plight may be of a lesser nature because of their mixed heritage.

And those two babies will not be with me this weekend because they are in foster care, because of a very strange set of circumstances. I hoped that Cutty had made some advances on his investigation, because Shea did not deserve to be held in jail, while a killer was walking around free. No, my baby needed to be released, and I

Cynthia Marlee Preston

was going to spend my weekend making sure that that would happen.

Chapter 19

Friday, January 26, 2001
6:00 PM

When I got home, Cutty was preparing a chicken stir-fry that smelled delicious. I remembered that I hadn't eaten all day and was just now getting hungry. He set the table and brought out a bottle of Chardonnay.

"How was your day, honey?" He asked me as we sat down to the table.

"It was bullshit. I accomplished nothing." I replied.

"How's Shea doing?" He asked.

"She is very upset" I responded, "Randall made it worse with his big mouth. Now he is threatening to take her away from me. And I won't get Mia and Michael until next week."

"Don't worry about Mia and Michael, right now. They are in good care. Now you have a few days to help me out with my business."

"What is your business, Cutty?"

"Trying to put this puzzle, together."

"What did you learn, today, hon?"

"Oh, baby. I learned some very interesting news. I learned that the Cuban Mafia has Franklin on lockdown. I learned that DJ Evans is dead!!! I learned that Bo and DJ attended a mob party on New Year's Day, together, and that Bo told Tammy that he was going to do business with them."

Cutty had his head extended toward mine when he said this, and caught my eyes in a lock.

"What do you suppose, Cutty?"

"I suppose the mafia was responsible, in some way, for the death of my brother, and your babies' daddy. What do you suppose?"

"I suppose you are probably right, Cutty. But, I have this nagging little voice that tells me that there is one player missing from the card game."

"And who would that be, Terry?" He asked.

"No clue, right now, babe. No clue. Just a feeling."

"Ok, honey. Let's take that feeling and try to make some sense of it." Cutty suggested. "Suppose DJ is Dante Johnson?"

"Now there's a leap. How do you figure?"

"DJ is dead. Dante Johnson is dead." Cutty reported.

"God, honey. I thought DJ Evans was just a street hustler? Now you are trying to tell me that DJ Evans was actually my babies' daddy, Dante?"

"Yes, I think he was, babe. A street hustler with mob ties. Dante was found dead on Franklin, where DJ lives, and DJ is dead."

"How does Bo fit into this?"

"Don't know, yet, but I will find out".

"Cutty, what do you know about the Cuban Mafia"?

"I did some work with them, years back. They're bad, baby, bad boys. They deal mostly in drug traffic and firearms. But they are politically active, as well. They own legitimate businesses in the Twin Cities, restaurants, real estate, and some marketing groups. They are fearless, and treacherous. When I was working for them, they killed a man who was getting too close to me."

"What??"

"Yeesssss! He was found in a bathtub, drowned, in a bathtub full of cocaine. The cocaine soaked into his pores and he had a heart attack and drowned."

"You are scaring me, now, Cutty."

"You should be scared, Terry. They are nobody to play with. You need to be careful, Lady, be very careful."

"What should we do?"

"First of all, do you have a picture of Dante that I could bring to Tammy?"

"Yes, of course. I have plenty of pictures of him with the kids."

"OK. Get a picture out for me and I will check it out with her. Secondly, I want you to try to get some information about businesses that the Cuban are running. You are the computer expert. Think you can research that?"

"I'll have to think about that one, Cutty. I'm sure I can figure out something."

"OK. I think that is all we can do, for now, baby. This is a more dangerous game that I first anticipated. We need to be careful and smart, baby. And remember, darlin', the MOUTH."

"Yes, dear", I replied, half listening after hearing the news, "the MOUTH."

Chapter 20

Friday, January 26, 2001
8:00 p.m.

After dinner, I fell asleep on the sofa and I had a strange dream:

I was responsible for a young girl, about six years old. She was very sweet and dear to me, but I didn't know who she was. I tucked her into my bed and was saying a children's prayer with her when a gray gust of wind broke the bedroom window, and came into the bedroom spinning like a tornado. It blew me over, picked up the little girl and spun right back out of the window with her inside the funnel. I looked out the window, but it was already out of sight.

I was screaming when a man in dazzling white robes and a glow emanating from him like liquid gold walked in through the bedroom door and took my hand in his. Just as I was about to leave with him, he turned into a huge monkey/human figure and attacked me with his claws and tried to bite me with his teeth.

Suddenly I could fly. I jumped up as high as I could and I was airborne. I flew out of the bedroom window and down the street to a fortune teller's house. I knocked on a door, and a black dog pushed the door open. Inside the house an old Chinese lady sat in a rocking chair.

"I'm frightened. Strange things are happening to me. A tornado stole my young girl and something strange is chasing me and trying to kill me". I shouted.

"What is it?" she asked.

"A monkey with huge claws and teeth." I replied.

"A monkey? A monkey, my dear, is known for its cunning. Did he trick you into believing that he was something other than a monkey?"

"Yes, actually, I thought he might be Jesus at first. He was in white robes and he had a liquid gold glow all around him."

"This sounds like a soul stealer, pure evil, son of the devil. You must kill this monkey beast. I have a special gun that I will give you to use."

"I don't know how to kill and I am afraid of guns. I hate guns." I had said it before, but this time I wasn't sure that I was telling the truth. I think my feelings had changed after handling Ellie's gun.

"Destroying evil should be second nature to a good woman." She emphasized the words evil and good.

"How should I know the difference between good and evil? I asked.

"You don't. Only your soul can discern good from evil. You learn to give everything in your life the truth test. If something can sit in your soul and you can live with yourself along side it, it is good. If something sits in your soul and your body starts bubbling to expel it, it is evil."

"I think I understand that. I rely on my inner instincts and feelings more than most people." I replied.

"That's probably why you were visited by both of them, the good savior and the evil destructive monkey. The fact that they were in one and the same body is also significant." She took a sip of tea and continued.

"Appearances have been deceiving since the beginning of time, dear. Remember the sweet red, juicy apple in the Garden of Eden? Remember the wooden horse of Troy, filled with an enemy army? Remember Eliphaz, Bildad, and Zophar, the self-righteous friends of Job, who judged him, blamed him and belittled him for disrespecting God? They claimed to know everything about the Most High until God himself appeared to them and called them hypocrites and fools."

"All of these people and situations appeared good until they were exposed." She explained.

"The Chinese culture attaches significance to people born each year by associating them with the animal that rules that year. What year were you born, dear?" She asked.

"1954." I replied. I already knew I was a horse.

"That makes you a horse. Actually, that makes you a wooden horse, just like the one in the story, with an army hidden inside. We all have forces within us for destruction and we all have forces within us for peace. Our job is to discern and act appropriately when we feel the dangers of life around us. Who is your worst enemy?"

"Probably my ex-husband." I responded, based on all the lawsuits he had tried to file against me.

"What year was he born?"

"1956."

"Ah, hah, I see now. The year of the monkey."

"What does that mean?"

Every Secret Thing

"You will figure it out. And what about your current lover? What year?"

"1960." I replied.

"The Rat!!! The leader of the animals. The first sign in the Chinese zodiac, but also the mortal enemy of the horse, until Yin and Yang is achieved, when it becomes a perfect union. Until that time, be wary of everyone. Rats can crawl up into places that you have never seen. A monkey can trick you and mock you."

"Tell me what to do? Please?"

"Don't ask for others to make your decisions for you. Make your own way. Now go and do what you need to do and let me rest. You will be o.k."

"Give me some advice, anyway."

"The best advice for you is this: the hands are the extensions of the heart. You can learn a lot through a person's hands. Look to the hands for keys to the soul."

She handed me a paint gun with some kind of a solution loaded inside of it. I left her house and headed home. The monkey sat on my front porch. I looked him square in the eye and fired the gun. He starting smoking and melting until he completely disintegrated. I walked up the stairs to the porch. There was nothing left but what looked like a spray painting of an American flag on the wooden porch floor. Alongside the flag was a fist, raised up in symbol of power.

I went through the front door into the house and found the little girl on the couch.

"Oh, my gosh. Thank God. Where did you go?" I asked her. I didn't even know her name.

"I went to see a man in white robes and gold glitter spraying off of him. He was nice to me." she replied.

When I looked down at her, I could see that her hands were exceptionally white and clean and that she wore a ring with a cross and three diamonds on it. It was just like my engagement ring.

"Baby", I said to the child. "Where did you get that ring?"

"He gave it to me, mommy".

"Sweetheart, I am not your mommy." I said.

"You are funny, mommy. My name is Shea Rebekah Onstad and I am six years old.!!!!"

"Oh, my gosh, my baby girl", I cried, and hugged her tight. "So much has gone wrong,

Every Secret Thing

Shea. I have been trying, but I know I have failed you."

"I'm glad you're here, mommy. I love you and you love me." She said, comforting me.

And then I awoke and my pillow was soaked and my eyes and heart were full.

Cynthia Marlee Preston

Chapter 21

Saturday, January 27, 2001
10:00 am

I slept in on Saturday morning and enjoyed the luxury of not being awakened by cartoons and kids jumping on my bed. Instead, I went to the computer room and logged on Netscape. I tried a search engine with two words, "rich" "Minnesotans". Several links popped up, but I chose one called "500 Richest Minnesotans."

The site was designed by name, net worth, businesses, rank. Each name was connected to a personal profile link. Each business was connected to a business profile link. I wasn't sure of what I was hoping to find, because I didn't know what I was looking for. Cuban name? Did I know any Cubans. The most famous Cuban I knew was Ricky Ricardo. I laughed out loud. I wondered if he had Mafia ties. No doubt, he did. Many entertainers, from that era, were promoted by the underground.

Underground? Businessmen without traditional offices? Or, maybe they did have offices, now. My knowledge of the mafia runs just short of Francis Ford Coppola's movies.

I looked at the names that came up on the 500 Richest Minnesotans list and started looking for

Every Secret Thing

the Latino names. There was an Ortiz, a Gutterez, a Martinez, and a Coronado. I double-clicked the mouse on Coronado.

A large picture of a smiling man with dark, wavy hair and thick, dark eyebrows, came up. Next to the picture was his biography.

"Emilio Coronado was born in Havana, Cuba on April 2, 1942. He came to Minnesota when he was 20. He and his brother, Ipolito, started up the Coronado Cabana on Nicollet in the early seventies. The Restaurant/Nightclub was very successful in its day, but has since closed and the brothers are now heavily invested in oil refineries, food and beverage companies, and restaurant equipment supplies. Their net worth exceeds 950 million dollars."

I backed out of the personal profile and double-clicked on the business profile.

"South Texas Refinery, Inc."
"Mid-west Refinery, Inc."
"Emil's Food and Beverage, Inc."
"Coronado Brother's Coffee and Tea"
"Gold Queen Food Equipment, Inc."
"Jack Sprat Low-fat Chicken, Inc."
"Palace Shipping and Handling, Inc."

Palace Shipping caught my eye. I went to the on-line directory to come up with their address. Within a second, the address and phone number popped up on my screen. 20156 Louisiana Ave. I wrote the address down. Cutty would have to make a trip over there.

Jack Sprat Low Fat Chicken sounded familiar, too. I was almost sure that Randall carried that product. Randall was in the food industry as a Sales Manager. I would have to make a call to him, today.

Chapter 22

Saturday, January 27, 2001
11:00 am

I called Cutty on his cell phone to ask him if he had ever heard of the Coronado brothers. He told me that he had heard their names in connection with the Cuban mafia. He also told me that Tammy had identified Dante as DJ Evans. I was stung by that revelation, even though Cutty had suspected it yesterday. Dante was a drug dealer and runner. I would have never expected such in a million years of knowing him. I guess you really can't trust anyone.

I gave Cutty the address of the shipping and handling company and he said that he would check it out. I told him to be careful and that I was going to call Randall to ask a few questions. We exchanged "I love yous" and hung up. I got right back on the phone to Randall.

"Hello" said Shandra, Randall's bride of six months.

"Is Randall there?" I asked.

"He's in his bedroom, lying down, trying to get rid of his sick headache." she replied.

"Well, get him for me, please." I demanded.

Randall always got sick headaches or backaches when Shea got into trouble. This rendered him helpless to assist me with her troubles. I could hear Shandra calling, "Randy, darling, telephone."

I wondered how long she would be calling him "darling". It lasted about eight months for me. The next nineteen years it was Randy, bastard.

"Hello?" I heard.

"Randall, this is Terry. I have a question for you."

"Shoot".

"Are you still selling Jack Sprat Low-Fat Chicken products?"

"What the hell? Don't we have more important things to discuss, like getting our daughter out of jail?"

"Yes, of course, Randall. Just wondering, on the chicken thing. Do you?"

"Yeah, we sell it. Why?"

"Do you know the owners?" I probed.

"I see them every year at the distributor's conference. What's it to you?"

"You said you wanted to talk about Shea, Randall? Why don't you come and pick me up and we can go to a neutral location to talk. That way, you can't holler at me."

"You MAKE me holler at you, Terry."

"Yes, I remember. Everything bad that you do is someone else's fault."

"You're a bitch, but we should talk. I'll pick you up at 2:30. Bye."

"Bye".

I put the phone down and went into the bedroom to get dressed. I was thinking about Dante, again. Dante and I had some wonderful times together. When times were good, we laughed and played like children.

I wonder what happens to love? It is so fleeting in so many relationships. I have had two major love relationships that went sour. I'm sad for that. I really don't believe that I ever loved Randall. I used to pray to God to increase my love for him. I just didn't feel it. That is why I became so infatuated with Dante. But I soon discovered that Dante was just a child, and I didn't need another child to care for.

I remembered what Shea told me about Stacy. How on earth did Stacy get herself messed up with Dante? She must be hurting if she felt she loved him. I felt bad that Stacy had put up a wall against me. I blamed Randall, completely for that mess.

I had so many thoughts pouring into my mind that I sat down on the bed and let my mind flow. If Dante was a drug runner, and Dante was with Stacy, then Stacy must know some information about the Cubans. I didn't even know where Stacy was living, now. I could ask Randall.

Dante's funeral. Where? When? Should I take the kids?

Who killed Dante? Who were the suspects? What was the motive? Greed? Jealousy? Drugs? Guns? Cutty thought Dante was trafficking cocaine. Was Dante using? Was Stacy using? How about Bo? Who killed Bo? Was Bo using? He was supposed to have been connected to the Cubans. Did he anger them? Did he slip up? Who would be next to die? Stacy?

A chill went right up my spine. Oh, my gosh. I've got to find her. These people are for real. Suddenly Cutty's warnings to me became real to me. "Be careful, Lady, be very careful".

Chapter 23

Saturday, January 27, 2001
2:00 pm

Cutty pulled up to the huge warehouse on Louisiana Ave. and parked in the empty lot. He got out of his car and slipped on a patch of ice, walking up to the side door. He caught himself before he fell, but the slip unnerved him a bit. He touched the door and tried the lock. It was open, to his surprise. He stamped the snow off of his feet, and pushed open the door.

He entered into a large, empty, dark warehouse. He removed his sunglasses and his gloves and then he looked up at the ceiling rafters. There was nothing, anywhere, in the warehouse. He started walking across the huge expanse, listening to his boots squish with each step on the cement floor. When he was about two-thirds of the way across the floor he was suddenly blinded by a floodlight, shining directly into his face. He raised his arm over his face, and tried to see what was happening. A microphoned voice filled the warehouse, just then: "You got business, here?" The male voice inquired.

Cutty could just make out a small room on the north side of the warehouse, up high. It reminded him of the film room at a movie house. He had to think fast and answer correctly, so he went on instinct.

"Yes. Yes, sir. I have business here." He replied.

"Where's the shipment?" The voice asked.

"It will be arriving soon", he said, "in the truck. I'm driving ahead and got here early. Just wanted to see the place. Looks like you got plenty of room."

"Is this Emilio's Chicago load?" he asked.

"Sir, could you please take that beam off my face?" Cutty asked.

"No. I asked you a question."

"Yes, sir, this is Emilio's Chicago load."

"He wasn't expecting a load this week. Who are you?"

Cutty heard the cock of a gun and looked for the nearest exit.

"I'm DJ Evan's assistant. I heard about the unfortunate death of DJ and brought the load in myself. I thought Mr. Coronado would be pleased. I was thinking that maybe he would be

Every Secret Thing

pleased enough to let me take DJ's territory." Cutty reported.

"Oh, I see. An opportunist, eh? Let me get Mr. Coronado on the telephone and see if he wants to work something out with you. Your name, please?"

"My name? You're asking me my name? Cutty stumbled for a moment.

"Yes, exactly. I am asking you, what is your name? Is that a problem?"

"My name is Enrico", Cutty bluffed.

"Good name, for a black man".

"Mixed blood. My mother was half Cuban".

"I see".

There was a long pause. Cutty vacillated between running now, for his life, or keeping up the game. His sense of adventure won, and he stayed. He waited quietly for 5 or 10 minutes.

"Mr. Coronado asks that you meet him at Subway on Franklin and Chicago. He said 4:00, and don't be late. You can go now, Enrico. I'll be awaiting the shipment and will let Mr. Coronado know when it arrives."

"Thank you, sir." Cutty walked back out the way he came in, hopped into his Cadillac, started the engine and drove like a bat out of hell. When he calmed down, he lit a cigarette, pulled over, parked and puffed on it until he got dizzy. Then he got on his cell phone and quickly called Terry.

Chapter 24

Saturday, January 27, 2001
2:30 p.m.

"Terry, I just went to the warehouse." Cutty said, breathless but excited. I bluffed and got in to see Emilio Coronado at 4:00 today."

"Cutty, I'm leaving to have a talk with Randall, but I want you to be careful with the Cubans. I'm worried that they may go after Stacy next."

"Why do you say that?"

"Because of her connection to Dante."

"Yeah, I think we can safely assume that a Cuban hit man killed Dante. I'm just surprised that he was running drugs in the first place. Why would he do that, Terry?"

"For the money, I guess. Money corrupts." I responded.

"Money makes the world go around, girl. We all want money in our lives."

"Yeah, Cutty. It is a double-edged sword. Nothing questionable about that. I guess I didn't know Dante as well as I thought I did." I replied.

"Don't doubt yourself, darlin'. What do you think was important to Dante?"

"His children." I responded, immediately.

"Then you are probably right, honey. Now go talk to Randall. And don't let that redneck asshole put you down. You are too good for that."

"Right. Randall doesn't know how to do anything but put a person down, but I will rise above it."

"There you go. Love you, Terry."

"I love you, too, Cutty. Be safe."

Chapter 25

**Saturday, January, 2001
2:45 p.m.**

When Randall arrived, I put on my leather coat and ran out to his car. The weather was changing. A wind had come up from the north and the sky was getting gray. I hopped into Randall's car and closed the door.

"You're still slamming doors, too hard," he said with some disgust.

"So what?" I responded.

"Where do you want to go? I'm not familiar with the ghetto."

"This isn't the ghetto, Randall. There is a Perkins down on Lake Street. Let's go there". I suggested.

We made the entire drive, in silence. We got to the restaurant, sat down and looked at the menus.

"Where is Stacy staying now?" I asked him.

"She is staying with Nathan."

"Oh, good. That's a good place for her". Nathan was her gay boyfriend whom she had known since she was 10.

"Do you have the address or phone number?" I asked.

"No. She usually calls me from her cell phone. I haven't been over to the apartment." He responded.

"Did you know that she was dating Dante?" I asked.

Randall's face got bright red. He looked at me with his eyes bulging.

"Who told you that?" He asked.

"A little bird." I replied.

"Your bird must be a cookoo bird." He responded.

"Randall, are you sure you don't know anything about this?" I could sense that Randall's discomfort was growing.

"My daughter would not date a nigger, unlike her slut mother."

"Ooh."

Every Secret Thing

We went back to reading our menus. I already knew what I was going to order. I folded my menu, and waited for the waitress. I looked around the restaurant and then back at Randall. I noticed a big gold ring on his finger. On the ring was a flag, filled in with diamonds, rubies and sapphires.

My God, is that thing real?" I asked.

"What?" He pulled his menu down.

I pointed to the ring.

"I don't wear fake anything", he replied with a pompous pride.

"It must have cost a fortune."

"No, just five grand", he replied. "You like it?"

Like it? My god, I thought it was hideous.

"Oh, —yeah. It's very nice. Very symbolic of your Patriot allegiances."

"Thank you." He responded, not understanding that I had just ridiculed him.

"What are you going to have, Randall?"

"The same thing I always have."

"Oh, yeah, Granny's Omelet." I had forgotten how dull he was. "Good choice. I think I will have a salad."

The waitress appeared and we ordered. Randall's cell phone rang.

"Hello. Yeah, we are having lunch right now. Your mother was just asking about you."

"Is it Stacy?" I broke into his conversation. "Let me talk to her."

"Stacy, your mother wants to talk to you". Randall put his hand over the receiver, "She doesn't want to talk to you", he replied with a smug look.

He continued listening and looking upset and concerned.

"No, Stacy. I don't want you driving to Chicago this weekend. The roads will be icy with this wind and we are supposed to get more snow tonight. Your little Eclipse is not a good winter car on the highway".

"Chicago", I said, "what does she plan to do in Chicago?"

Randall held the receiver, again. She says that she got tickets to the Dave Matthew's Band

Every Secret Thing

and wants to go with Beth and Nathan, driving in her car."

"No, way." I whispered to Randall.

"Ok, Stacy, go ahead. Just be careful and call me when you get there. Bye, honey. I love you".

"I love her, too. Tell her."

"Too late, she hung up!"

Bastard.

"So you let her go, huh?" I asked.

"She is 20 years old. I can't stop her."

"Well, Shea is 15 and you can't stop her from living with me when she has decided that my home is her home."

"Oh, yes, there is. I've got pages of notes on what a bad mother you are, starting with the fact that you would bring a ghetto gangster nigger into your home and shack up with him under the same roof that protects my daughter." Randall's face was alive with hatred and anger.

"You're wrong, Randall. We are a family. Patrick and I are engaged to be married. Shea loves Patrick like a father and he has done a tremendous job settling her down while you've done nothing but lay in bed with sick headaches when she is in trouble. You don't pay me any child support, you never visit her and she won't go to your house, 'cause you usually have some dumbass hoe shacking up with you. And cut the racial profanity, please. It offends me!!"

Randall stood up, threw his napkin down, threw his lukewarm coffee on me and shook his fist at me.

"You, bitch". He screamed at the top of his lungs. "You fuckin' bitch"

"Quiet, Randall, sit down." I whispered, loudly.

By this time, the people in the restaurant were talking and staring. I was horrified and Randall stormed out of the restaurant, leaving me, one more time, all alone with a mess to clean up.

Chapter 26

**Saturday, January 27, 2001
4:00 p.m.**

Cutty got a full description of the restaurant incident when he finally reached Terry, by phone.

"It isn't like Randall to lose his cool in public, Cutty. His behavior, in a private setting, wouldn't have been surprising, but he is so image conscious in public. He has a hatred toward you that scares me."

It wouldn't be the first time someone hated me for dating their ex-girlfriend or ex-wife", Cutty replied, calmly. "Anyway, I have to get into this Subway store and meet Coronado."

"Cutty, you're taking this thing too far, on your own. I say you forget it, now. We'll let the police solve it."

"Lady, the police are probably taking a slice of the Coronado brother's pie. They aren't going to do a thing to solve it. Gotta go, now."

Cutty turned off his cell phone and walked into the Subway shop. Sitting, in the corner, was the same man Cutty had seen on Franklin, yesterday, the oldest of the three. As Cutty approached him, he stood up and reached out for Cutty's hand.

Cutty took it and shook it, surprised by the softness and fine features of the perfectly manicured hand.

"Enrico? Or, is it Big C?"

Cutty laughed and pointed his finger at him, in that "you got me" gesture.

"Call me C, Mr. Coronado."

"Ok, Ok." He looked Cutty over and nodded his head. "You look like a very strong man, C. Now, tell me what is it that you do?"

"I'm unemployed. I tried taking the straight and honest path, but the white man kicked me to the curb and put me back on the street. I need a good hustle. What I want from you is the Chicago/Minneapolis run, recently vacated, I understand."

"Oh, yes. Terribly unfortunate, Mr. Evan's demise. Were you a close friend, Mr. C?"

"Yes, very close, very sad", he replied.

"Yes, then you must have been as surprised as we were to learn that DJ Evans was an undercover cop." Emilio Coronado stared Cutty straight in the eyes.

Every Secret Thing

Cutty could feel the blood draining right out of his face. He said nothing, but his mind was as calculating and cunning as the old man's.

"I suspected such. This is the first confirmation I have had, on that matter."

"Yes, Mr. C. I see. Then, I suppose you must understand that the Chicago and Minneapolis police are all over his murder."

Cutty's mind was racing. Private. Secret. Words Terry often used to describe Dante.

"This mean's that we have to be especially careful, right now. I was told that you had a shipment coming in; that you were bringing it in for DJ?"

"I can detour that shipment for a while, if necessary", Cutty responded.

"Yes, I think that would be wise. The warehouse is clean and we would like to keep it that way until the dust settles.

"I'll get right on it, Mr. Coronado." Cutty bluffed.

"By the way, Mr. C, the dust will settle just fine. You can believe that we have our connections in high places with the cities of Chicago and

Minneapolis police departments. I will be in touch." Emilio responded.

"Do you want my cell number?" Cutty offered.

"We have it, Mr. C."

Cutty wasn't surprised by the fact that they had done their homework on him. He stood up and shook Emilio's hand, again. This time Emilio squeezed his small hand tightly around Cutty's and stared him in the eyes.

"I believe that you have something of mine!" Coronado said.

"What would that be?" Cutty asked, surprised.

Emilio reached into Cutty's breast pocket on his coat and pulled out the gold sunglasses.

"I'll take these, back." He said.

Cutty walked out of the Subway and into the dusky January afternoon.

Chapter 27

Saturday, January 27, 2001
6:00 p.m., Coronado Home

Emilio and Ipolito Coronado sat together with their associates at the dinner table in Emilio's home. They were being served a lobster bisque with bread and olive oil, when they started discussing the Cutter affair.

"You know he is the brother of Bo Preston, do you not, Emilio?" Ipolito asked his brother.

"Listen, Ipolito, Bo's blood is not on our hands. We still don't know who took him out, or why. That is still a puzzlement to me and I don't like it." Emilio responded to his brother.

"Brother, when a man dies on the street like that, chased and shot in the head, it is anybody's guess. It could have been a jealous husband, a drug incident, a stolen car, anything." Ipolito explained.

"Bo Preston was a handsome man, and strong, like his brother. But he had a mouth on him. He wanted to be top dog, too soon. I think his mouth got him killed. He didn't have back-up, like I understand his brother has. Yes, Patrick Cutter is affiliated with the G.D.'s, Gangster Disciples." Emilio reported.

"Damn, brother, we don't need that kind of trouble, now. Things are too hot already, after taking DJ Evans out. By the way, Egg, good job on Evans, very clean."

"Thanks, boss." Egg Travino was a hit man, big, fast and effective. "I didn't like it that his girl was with him at the time. She darted out of the scene before I knew it. Tall, blonde girl. Modelish type. I don't think she's dangerous. Just scared."

"Not to worry, Egg." Ipolito assured him.

"So what are we going to do with Big C Cutter?" Egg asked.

"We are going to let him have the Chicago/Minneapolis route. We can set him up with a railroad job and get him to ship from the RR until the streets are clean again." Emilio answered.

"Brilliant idea, brother." Ipolito said with pride.

"If we find he isn't straight, we take him out, just like DJ. Egg knows the protocol, don't you Egg". Emilio said.

"Sure, boss. Just let me know." Egg replied.

"Yes, I will let you know. I'm quite sure he is in it to find out what happened to his brother. After that, he skips or informs. Mark my words." Emilio said, thoughtfully.

"Let's eat. Maria, bring out the Porterhouse steaks, please and some of my best red wine for my family and friends."

Chapter 28

Saturday, January 27, 2001
5:00 p.m.

Cutty was rolling again in his Caddy on Franklin. He went back to Terrell Cox's door and rang the bell. Cox came down with a light skinned black man.

"I got some word on DJ, Big C. This here is one of his homies, Humpty."

"How you doing, Humpty." Cutty bumped fists with him.

"Hey, man." Humpty replied.

"Big C, I need some cash, man. Pay me for some information on Bo." Cox begged.

"Let me hear what you got first. I'll pay you what its worth."

Cox nodded at Humpty.

"Dogg, DJ just came to town a few months ago." Humpty started.

"Don't call him Dogg, man. He ain't no dog." Cox told Humpty.

Every Secret Thing

Cutty nodded at Cox and looked back at Humpty who was looking a little surprised.

"OK, man. DJ told me he was one of the Evan's brother's cousins from Chicago. Said he was here to locate a man named Patrick Cutter, from St. Paul, who had fucked up on a check cashing scam."

"Is that right?" Cutty replied with some anger in his voice. "Go on." Cutty folded his arms across his chest.

"No one here had ever heard of Patrick Cutter, but someone hear of a Bo Preston from St. Paul who had been hanging out on Franklin selling small time chronic, mostly. It was revealed that this was Patrick Cutter's brother. DJ asked the brother to point him out."

"When was that?" Cutty asked.

"Thanksgiving time?" Humpty told Cutty.

"Anyway, DJ met Bo and worked with him for a while and then connected Bo with the Coronado brothers on New Year's Day. Bo was starting to dress fine and bought hisself some gold chains. He was smoking up most of his cash, though. Got the tongue for the rock."

"Sounds like my brother." Cutty affirmed.

"Well, DJ's woman lived in number one, here, Stacy something. She was hot, dogg, very hot."

"Dogg?" Cox broke in.

"Sorry, Mr. C. Anyway, Stacy did not fit into the picture very well. She obviously a polished girl from the suburbs. Bo liked her long legs. She stood up taller than DJ. She drove a black Eclipse Spider. One night, Bo took it for a ride, without permission. Got hisself in trouble with Dante. He left the car parked on Lake Street the night he got killt. But not until he had picked up his woman from work and taken her for a spin. She axt him where he getting a car and clothes and money.

Anyway, we see two cars driving around later that night. One was DJ's car, a Monte Carlo, and the other was a black Lincoln with tinted windows. We figure it the Cubans. We all hanging low, knowing something is going down. But nobody around when the shot is fired. Nobody see him chased. Nobody see him shot. DJ come out about 10:00 that night and we connected about 1:00, just before the murder is reported. We standing on the sidewalk watching homicide do their thing. DJ looks upset and nervous."

"Did DJ know how to use a gun?"

"DJ was military, man. He know how to fire, but I never seen him use a gun. I never even seen him carry."

"Where was DJ's girl during all this?" Cutty asked.

"She inside her place. All the lights on, anyway. That about all I know, Mr. C. Since that time, everything been dry and DJ been hanging low. His girl move out and on Tuesday night, DJ shows up dead on the street. We seen Coronado around a few times, walking Franklin, like he looking for clues, picking up shit off the streets."

"Humpty, Shorty. You've been very helpful." Cutty handed each of them a hundred-dollar bill and went back to his Cadillac.

Chapter 29

Saturday January 27, 2001
8:00 PM

Tasha was home alone when Cutty arrived. "Where is Terry?" he asked.

"She went over to visit Granny." Tasha replied. "She was pretty angry with Shea's dad.

"Any phone calls?" Cutty asked.

"Yeah. The Police called to say the bullet found in Dante did not match the gun in the closet. Shea's going to be released tomorrow."

"Does Terry know?"

"Yeah, she was the one who took the call. Now they are going to check to see if the bullet from Bo's head matches the gun?"

"Tasha?"

"Yes, Dad?"

"I love you."

"I love you, too, dad." Tasha turned back to the television, and wondered what his problem was tonight!

Chapter 30

Saturday, January 27, 2001
9:00 p.m.

When Cutty called his mother's house, his voice was calm and subdued.

"Hi, mom." He said.

"Hello, son." She replied.

"How's Terry?" He asked.

"She's fine. Just a little shaken over all the events in the past few days."

"Yeah, me too." Cutty replied.

"Me, three." Ellie laughed.

"Mom, I think Bo was killed by Terry's babies' father."

"Ellie thought on that for a few moments.

"I don't think so, Patrick."

"Why not?"

"It doesn't sit right in my gut."

"What does sit right in your gut, mom? You can't eat pork, you can't drink milk, and you can't season your catfish the way you like it."

Ellie laughed.

"Patrick, let's just put it on hold for the night. O.K.?

"O.K., mom. Tell Terry that I love her."

"She'll be home soon, son. Give her a few hours of peace with me."

"Gotcha. Bye, mom. I love you."

"Give Tasha my love, son, and take care of your nasty self. I love you, too, even though you make me mad, sometimes. You sho' do make me mad." And with that Ellie hung up the phone.

Chapter 31

Stacy

Stacy Onstad was 20 years old. She had been one of those "wunderkinds"; children who amazed their parents with their advanced knowledge, skills and maturity, from a very young age. In Stacy's case, she was playing the piano, figuring out complex math problems, and writing stories by the age of five.

I was always acutely aware of my responsibility to keep Stacy's inquisitive mind as stimulated as possible. A gifted child makes a mother feel like a teacher more than a mother. She has to continue to remind herself that this is a little girl who needs to be hugged and played with as much as the child resists those advances.

As Stacy grew into a young teen, I could sense a major problem growing in my household. Randall was threatened by Stacy's intellect and would stifle her voice when she would assert an opinion that was contrary to his. His method of stifling her was to glare at her with an angry stare, his eyes bugging out of their sockets, a vein popping out of his forehead and then holler at her in a belittling and disrespectful way. This would send Stacy fleeing from the dinner table in tears of anger and embarrassment.

Cynthia Marlee Preston

I was thoroughly disgusted that a grown man would try to weaken his daughter's self-development, including her need to examine society and herself.

Stacy wasn't surprised when I left her father. My mistake was that I didn't have him removed from my home, but rather fled from him in fear of my safety. He had discovered that I was having an affair with Dante. I went to my brother's house, and while I was there, Randall was using Stacy as his grief counselor. He gave her intimate details of our love life and read to her my journal involving intimate details of my love affair with Dante.

Stacy later told me that it made her sick every time her father would ask her to take a ride in the car with him. That meant that he would sob and tell her disturbing details of adult life at its worst. I still feel guilty, to this day, for not having been there to protect both of my daughters from the worst kind of abuse that their own father was perpetrating, to his total ignorance.

Shea was told that I didn't want my old family anymore. Stacy was told the same, and given a vulgar picture of her mother. The girls were 10 and 15 at the time, and I should have kicked the bastard out of the house with a court order, rather than turning and running on my own behalf. God forgive me for my selfishness.

Chapter 32

**Sunday, January 28, 2001
3:00 a.m.**

Stacy Onstad sat in the Chicago police station in Detective Burns' office. It was 3:30 a.m. She was crying.

"How could you let Dante get killed? I was with him when he was shot. It was terrible". She sobbed.

"I'm sorry, Stacy." He handed her another Kleenex." Now tell me exactly what the man who shot him looked like."

"He was big. Covered up in a big coat. Hat on. It was hard to see his face. He looked dark. Not black, but Hispanic, I think. I think he was one of the Cubans".

"Did he say anything"?

"Yes, he called his name. He called him DJ."

"Did he get a good look at you?"

"No. He glanced at me right before I ran. He didn't try to follow me."

"That's good, Stacy. Now tell me what Dante had been doing. We hadn't heard from him for a while."

"Well, he had made a connection with Bo Preston on New Year's Day. Bo was causing Dante some trouble. I think Bo had become suspicious of Dante. He was talking trash to him on several occasions. Dante would bring in the load and Bo would deal it. Bo was also using. I think he might have been blaming Dante for bringing in a short shipment, when he was actually using the missing product."

"I, see." Detective Burns, replied. "We got word from the Minneapolis police on the ballistics report on the gun that was found at the Onstad house. It was not the gun that was used to kill Dante. That means that they will be releasing your sister, today."

"Thank, God. That was all craziness, anyway."

"Not, necessarily. They are going to run it through to see if it was the gun that killed Bo?"

"Cutty would not kill his brother." Stacy replied, emphatically.

"We always check out family on these things, Stacy".

Every Secret Thing

"Well, I want out of all this. I wish I had never gotten messed up in this in the first place. I shouldn't have been with Dante, and I don't want to continue in this mess. I'm scared. My dad would kill me if he knew what I was doing. I can't talk to my mom because I am too ashamed of myself." She put her head in her hands and sobbed.

"Stacy, I don't expect that we will need you, anymore. We are all mourning the loss of Dante. I have been talking to his parents every day. They didn't know anything about his activities, and now he is dead. They want to see the babies, your brother and sister. Maybe you could help out your mother with getting them to Chicago for the funeral. It might be that chance you need to heal some wounds with your mother."

Stacy looked up, feeling better, suddenly. "Yes, that's good. That is a good idea."

When Stacy left the office, Detective Burns notified Minneapolis headquarters that he believed that he had solved the murders of Bo Cutter and Dante Johnson. He explained that Dante had a motive for wanting Bo dead, because he feared that Bo might blow his cover as an undercover cop, and he had been in Terry Onstad's home on January 22 with Terry's daughter Stacy and he would have been able to plant the gun at that time. He explained that Dante had been found out by the mob and taken out by one of their hit men. They would never get to the bottom of that story and might as well close the books as a mob hit.

When he hung up the phone, he poured himself a scotch from his bottom drawer and stretched out in his chair. After a few moments, he put in one final call to Emilio Coronado to tell him the good news.

Chapter 33

Sunday, January 28, 2001
9:00 a.m.

Cutty and I had our coffee in the sunroom. I was marinating in the good news from the Juvenile Detention Center that Shea would be released at noon. I was overwhelmingly relieved and I was chattering on to Cutty, the way I do when life is looking good again, after a downward spiral. Cutty was feeling good, too, both about Shea's release and the way that he felt he had outsmarted the Coronado group.

Cutty was leaning back in the wicker armchair with his legs outstretched, his head resting on the large fan shaped chair back. He resembled an Egyptian king with his slanted, slit eyes and his powerful wide set cheekbones glistening in the morning sun. One elbow was resting on the chair arm while his fingers explored the past day's beard growth on his chin. The other arm rested comfortably on the arm of the chair.

"What are you dreaming about, babe?" I asked.

"Nothing. I'm just enjoying some peace and some calm. It's a beautiful morning. Look how the birds are snatching sunflower seeds out of the snow, after that nasty old squirrel swung on the bird feeder and spilled the seed all over the ground. They all being greedy, especially old Mr. Squirrel with his cheeks full of seed all the way back to his ears. Kinda like life on the streets; everyone waiting for a spill so that they can gather up some riches for a few moments in time."

"Yes it is." Cutty was just getting warmed up, I could tell.

"The Coronado brothers are going to let me run for them, I believe; but, they won't trust me. They'll be watching my every move. I am going to have to play this out very carefully. Emilio's sunglasses were dropped on the street where DJ Evans lived, and where Bo was killed. I think that he was behind the murder of DJ, but I still don't know what to make of Bo's death? It's haunting me, Terry. I hear his voice crying out to me. He was my little brother and I wasn't there when he needed me. I won't rest until I find out who killed him and bring that man to justice.

I thought about Cutty's words and I did understand his feelings.

"I understand, honey, but at what price to you? To your mother? To your children? And to me? The people that love you, babe, do not want to see you get killed.

Every Secret Thing

"Big C is too smart to get killed." He answered, believing every word.

"Big C is your soul, babe. That is why you feel so indefatigable. Because you put your soul out there on the street, and God is in your soul. But your flesh, baby, is just that: FLESH. Bullets can penetrate the flesh, but not the soul. All I am saying is be careful. I love you and a lot of people are counting on you."

Cutty turned to me and smiled.

"You are an exquisite woman, Terry."

Wow, those were words that I would cherish, forever. I know my face lit up like a lamp. It's funny. When you have lived with an insecure man for so long, like I did with Randall, you had to learn to compliment yourself. He wouldn't compliment you, for fear of putting you up higher than him.

Cutty's surety of purpose and mind allowed him the freedom to love and praise others. I felt so lucky to be on the receiving end of that kind of love. Blessed to be a Blessing, as the Bible says, is a wonderful truth and the foundation of man's love. I was very blessed to have a man like Cutty in my life. I had hoped that I was a blessing to him, too, and now, with just a few delicious words, he confirmed that for me.

Cynthia Marlee Preston

We both sat in silence, drinking our coffee and looking at the winter landscape. The sky was clear and the sun was coming up bright at its January angle. The January angle in Minnesota is that time of the year when the sun rises and sets on the edge of the earth. I get a little claustrophobic because it feels like the sun isn't tall enough. I want the sun to be right over my head at noon. Instead, I can see my shadow at noon because of the angle of the sun.

I love sun and moon folklore and truths. Like the story of how an egg will sit upright by itself on the day of the spring solstice; or, how most babies are born under a full moon. The moon had a generous imagery surrounding it. The fuller the moon, the more the life-force and emotion of the earth and its inhabitants. Oceans would swell, crazy people would do crazy things, imaginary evils, like werewolves would come to life, babies would sprout from the womb, and eggs would stand alone, as if they were able to walk away on their own limbs.

The sun had a more miserly imagery. Icarus, flying too high on his wax wings and the sun melting the wax, plunging the Greek god to his demise. The sun, holding its warmth in the winter, and baring its heat in the summer, to the powerless populous below; the sun and the moon passing, causing total darkness to the day; the sun, looking for holes in the ozone, to wreak havoc on the earth; the sun, flaring in anger would someday bake the earth into non-existence. The sun was a tyrant; the moon, a populist.

Yet, despite these rulers of the earth, there is an even greater ruler of man who let's us know how vain our earthly endeavors are in his eyes. "Vanity of vanities," saith the Preacher, "vanity of vanities; all is vanity. What profit hath a man of all his labour which he taketh under the sun?"

Street hustlers are no less sinful or blessed than evangelists; but, it is the duty of man to do right and fear God. To do right, laws must be obeyed and the commandments of God must be upheld within those laws. People were being killed on one of our streets. Human rights were being violated; young lives were being adversely affected; family lives were being devastated. Wrongs needed to be righted. For that reason, alone, I started to believe in Cutty's mission to bring to justice the persecutors and I decided not to mention fear or caution to him again, as a deterrent to his goals.

"For God shall bring every work into judgment, with every secret thing, whether it be good, or whether it be evil."

Cynthia Marlee Preston

Chapter 34

Sunday, January 28, 2001
12:00 Noon

When I got to the Juvenile Detention Center, I was met by Randall and his attorney. They asked me to enter a conference room.

Randall's attorney had been a staple in his life since we separated. I could never understand how he could afford to keep him on retainer. Randall made good money, but I had been receiving weekly letters from Ross Lorentz, of Hart, Lorentz and Serento for years.

The letters would speak to specific details of my private life, comments I was alleged to have spoken, actions that I was alleged to have made. I was told in the letters to refrain from this or refrain from that, when I had never done "this" or "that" in the first place.

I was accused of the vilest actions. At first I tried to fight everything. Finally, Cutty told me to rip up the letters and not to ponder on them. It was the best advice that I ever received. My blood pressure dropped and my sanity returned.

As I thought about it now, I understood that they had done two things: 1) they had painted a terrible picture of me through their lies, insults and

Every Secret Thing

innuendos, documented by one-sided letters, and 2) they had robbed me of my freedom and my reputation.

"What is going on, Randall?" I asked, breaking the silence.

The very patronly Mr. Ross Lorentz laid out a legal order in front of me, signed by a judge, which stated four findings of fact:

1) Shea Onstad was in danger in my care because she had a record of police arrests. (There was no explanation of these arrests having occurred over a year ago)
2) Shea Onstad was neglected in my care because she was not attending public school. (No mention of home school)
3) Shea Onstad was in danger because a known felon was living with me. (No explanation of the fact that Cutty had had no arrests in 10 years)
4) Shea Onstad should immediately be turned over to her father, and her father should have sole custody of her.

I read the order and felt the fear engulf me. It was a temporary order, until such time as an evidentiary hearing could be scheduled, but I already knew the verdict. Legal bias had already claimed me unfit. It would now be my fight to defend myself, my beliefs, my ethics, my unconventional lifestyle to a system that was biased against divorced women and toward rich, white men.

Something broke apart within me at that moment. It started in my throat and tumbled down into the inner recesses of my stomach. It left a gaping hole and a tremendous fear that started my whole body trembling. Tears flowed from my eyes and sent me into choking sobs and deep moans of a sound that I had never heard before, like an animal howling.

My baby was brought into the room and Randall and two guards whisked her out the door just as she screamed for me to help her.

I sat in that room for a long time. No one came in to console me. I sat alone, in that room until my head cleared and my eyes flashed a permanent picture of that experience into my brain. For the first time in my life, I understood why you can't trust anyone but God. Where was my God at that moment? He was in a puff of oxygen in the upper chamber of my heart. He got in, as the helium was let out. My pride was destroyed.

Randall was no Savior for Shea. On the contrary, Randall had lived in relationships with three different women since our divorce. I believed he had brought the women into our house to be there for Shea while he was out traveling and drinking with his clients and other women on the road. These 'babysitters' believed that Randall loved them and planned to marry them.

One of them, Brandy, came to me for consolation after Randall told her that she was going to have to move out for a while because he was going to file for custody and child support from me and that she couldn't be living at the house while the Guardian ad Litem was researching custody arrangements. He moved her into an apartment and moved another woman into the house the next week. He asked the new matronly, heavyset woman to marry him and they visited with the Guardian ad Litem, together. When he was denied sole custody and child support from me, he blamed her and kicked her to the curb.

Randall was a racist man with severe paranoia, uncontrollable anger and lack of good judgment, as was displayed when he used his 15 year old daughter as a grief counselor when I left him. I believed him to be a very mean, greedy and ugly man, not to mention a bad father and I felt terrible that Shea was going to have to live with him.

But Randall had his "image" to protect him; his shoe shining, Franklin Planner toting, Lincoln Town Car driving, Ralph Lauren wearing image. When you stripped everything away, Dante, Cutty and Randall were all the same man.

Cynthia Marlee Preston

They were all only (or oldest) sons who were conceived by single mothers, who never knew their fathers, who had learned survival on the streets, who were high achievers with perfectionist tendencies and who enjoyed hard work and thrived on recognition.

Randall had climbed the ladder of success. Dante and Cutty kept stepping on broken rungs. Randall had no schooling after grade 12. Dante and Cutty had military experience and post-secondary schooling. Randall was a white man. Dante and Cutty were black men.

This is what I pondered that day.

Every Secret Thing

Chapter 35

Sunday, January 28, 2001
2:00 p.m.

Instead of going home, I drove out of the city. My second home was a little town in northern Minnesota and I needed to connect with something that felt nice and clean and real. The road was covered with ice and snow, so I had to drive slow and easy.

The landscape of the Red River Valley is very flat. Along Interstate 94 the land is speckled with farmhouses, each with at least one tall silo rising up against the blue winter skies. It projects a very lonely image, as does the long stretch of highway without another car for miles. As life imitates art, so families imitate environment and I am aware of the lonely and stoic pain of isolation that echoes from these homes.

My home is on a lake, further north and nestled within a forest and its creatures: deer, owls, squirrels, skunks and chipmunks. I was anxious to arrive at the lake, because I knew I could clear my thoughts at that time.

Randall was always trying to throw a curve ball my way. I wasn't surprised by his antics, just irritated by them. He had to interfere anytime opportunity knocked. I was convinced that his

Cynthia Marlee Preston

primary motivation in life was to get back at me for leaving him in such a humiliating way, pregnant with a black man's baby.

I arrived at the summer home, now covered with icicles and a thick coating of heavy snow on the roof. I dug for my key and let myself in to the chilly house. I could see my breath all around me. The sun was emblazoned on the western windows as it was slowly sinking behind the broad expanse of frozen lake.

I turned up the furnace and ran out back to get some firewood before dark. While near the shed I checked on my snowmobile. I put the key in the ignition and fired it up.

"Vroom-Vroom", it started and then purred like a big fat satisfied cat in the sunshine. I turned off the motor and left the keys in the ignition. I'd take it for a spin, later on.

I opened up the circuit box and turned on the electrical to the sewer and hot water heater. I brought in a load of wood, went down to the cellar and turned on the water. When I came back up, the house was already warming nicely. I closed the back door and kicked off my snowy boots.

The fireplace always scared me after a period of abandonment. You could never tell what you might find when you opened the flue. One time a bat fell down from the chimney and was flapping

Every Secret Thing

about inside and sticking to the glass door, squealing as it melted on the glass. Suddenly, as though it had a second life, it pulled itself away from the glass door, flapped its wings through the flames and escaped up the chimney to freedom. I saw it flying toward a tree out of my front picture windows.

Fortunately nothing fell as I turned the opening today. I balled up some newspaper and stuck it under the crate. Then I criss-crossed some small sticks as a nest and laid three birch logs on top.

"Poof" – a fire was born with a big, long wooden match. Making a good fire brought me a feeling of skill and success. A proud accomplishment.

I sat down on the living room couch and switched on the television just in time to catch the nightly news. The top story was about an activist group that had become undone and was now taking the law into its own hands. They were an anti-government force, now holed up in a secluded farmhouse and threatening the local police with their firearms and explosives. The FBI had been called in, and were presently surrounding the farm.

In this northern wildlife setting, the people were as wild about their beliefs as the animals around them were about collecting food this time of year. There had been a group of abortion rights protesters who had held vigil for twenty years, on a small public health clinic. Neither the clinic, nor the protesters had won the battle, and the battle continued raging, to this day.

As I sat there watching this report, I started questioning where these people get their guns, ammunition and explosives? They are run, I suspected, just like drugs are run, from a supplier in a larger city. They are probably dropped off in warehouses and transported throughout the state by dealers and salesmen. They probably used people in respectable jobs to run these items. Someone like Cutty would draw too much attention to himself.

I knew that the Coronados were into firearm trafficking. I expected that with their chain of businesses and warehouses, they were able to create all the links necessary for distribution. Suddenly, a picture of Randall's hand popped into my mind's eye, creating a link that I never would have come to make on my own.

"Look to the hand for clues to the soul." The old lady in the dream had advised.
Randall's strange ring, his sudden wealth, his lawyer, always hanging at the other end of his cell phone, his origination from this region, his current employment distributing one of the Coronado's products, Jack Sprat's Lowfat Chicken.

Every Secret Thing

If Randall had access to the Coronado's warehouse, he might have also come in contact with some of the drug trafficker's too, like Bo Preston and Dante. Maybe Randall had been at that New Year's Eve party at the Coronados. Maybe he saw Dante there with Bo.

Randall knew Dante and hated him. Dante might have feared that Randall would blow his cover. They might have conspired, together, being that they each had a secret to keep. Bo Preston might just have overheard this conspiracy and threatened to blackmail them, giving them a motive to kill Bo. Bo was shot dead on January 6, 2001. Dante was shot dead on January 24, 2001. Only one of these three men was still alive... Randall!!!

Chapter 36

Monday, January 29, 2001
9:00 a.m.

Cutty woke up to a message on his cell phone, inviting him to a cocktail party at the home of Emilio Coronado, that evening. Cutty wondered what was up with a Monday night cocktail party. Sounded to him like damage control. The phone rang again as Cutty stood stretching his body in his morning routine.

"Hell-o", he answered.

"Terry Onstad, please." The voice asked.

"She's not home right now." Cutty responded.

"Is this Patrick Cutter?"

"Yes".

"Patrick, this is Minneapolis Homicide Detective, Paul Richards. I'm working the case on your brother Bo's murder. The ballistics report confirms that the gun found in Mrs. Onstad's home, and the bullet found in your brother's head are a match. So now, we have our first good lead on your brother's murder."

Every Secret Thing

"That's good, Detective Richards, very good news. My mother will be pleased. Now, Paul, I hope that those of us who live here are not suspects, because none of us has any motivation to kill my brother." Cutty said.

"Mr. Cutter, I believe exactly as you say. I've done backgrounds on all of you, and I just don't see it. I don't feel it, either. I think we've got some bigger fish in the tank, don't you, Mr. Cutter?"

"Yes, detective, I know we got some sharks in the tank."

"Can we work together on this, Mr. Cutter?"

"Yes, we can work together."

"Mr. Cutter?"

"Call me Cutty, man."

"Ok, Cutty. Tell me what you think is going down?"

"I think the Cubans killed Dante." Cutty replied.

"Yeah, I can believe that. The shot came from a long distance and it was clean through the head. But Bo's shot was sloppy. No sign of professionalism there." Detective Richards responded.

"How about a theory that one of the Cuban's runners held a grudge and took matters into their own hands?" Cutty suggested.

"Now we're on the same sheet of music, Cutty. Any clues?"

"Damn, I've been off the streets so long."

"Cutty, what was your very first instinct when you heard that your brother was dead?"

"Blackmail killing. Bo had a way of finding dirt on people and extracting money from them."

"OK!!! This is helpful. Cutty, the Cubans have got all kinds of white collars running arms for them. They use their companies to find sympathizers of anti-government causes. They call themselves "Patriots", a misnomer, but a reality. They are really the U.S. version of terrorists."

"Is that so?" Cutty reflected.

"What's more interesting is the surprising number of men and women who allow themselves to get involved with this group, simply through greed. They are recruited by the company for sales jobs but they look for a certain profile

Every Secret Thing

through the job application process. Have you ever been asked to fill out one of those interest tests as part of a job search process?"

"Yeah, the one where they ask you what you like to do and what you don't like to do?" Cutty asked.

"Yes, that's it? Well, they analyze these tests, and then, after a respectable period of time they have a controlled conversation in the break room, with one company man playing the true redneck while cameras record the reactions of the other. This is how they find the true sympathizers. They also run background checks and credit checks on all of their employees, to find their employees' weak spots. Financial problems are the best motivator. You would be surprised to find out how easy it is to turn your everyday Joe, into a felon, overnight."

"No, I wouldn't be surprised at all. I've been seeing it my whole life!" Cutty replied.

"Anyway, I've been suspecting this Randall Onstad character. Makes a lot of money, but spends it faster than he can make it. I've been checking him out. Fits the redneck profile like a glove. What I don't know, is how dangerous he is outside of the network. Would he kill? I'm suspecting him in your brother's murder, and when you say that Bo had a propensity for blackmail, I might not be too far off the mark with

Onstad." Detective Richards stated, and then continued.

"Onstad's got ego problems. If he is made to look bad, he becomes enraged. I've talked to some of the secretaries in the department. You can get a pretty good analysis of a man's disposition, by the company's receptionist."

"Just like you can get right down to the heart of a pimp through his hoes." Cutty laughed back.

"Where's Terry?" Detective Richards asked.

"No clue". Cutty replied. "She went to pick up Shea yesterday at noon, and never came home. I called the detention center and found out that Shea was forced to go with her dad. I'm guessing that Terry is off licking her wounds, right now."

"So where would Terry go to lick her wounds?" The detective asked.

"A hotel, a bar or her lake home up north." Cutty knew his woman pretty well. "A hotel if she wants to lose herself in luxury, a bar, if she wants to lose herself in the bottle, and the lake home if she wants to think."

"I want a watch put out on her until we get her ex-husband checked out. Is there a phone at the lake?"

Every Secret Thing

"No. She either lost her cell phone or the battery is dead. I can't reach her."

"Then I'll dispatch a car from the closest town. What is it close to?"

"Pelican Rapids. I'll go myself." Cutty insisted.

"No, Cutty. I need you here to work with Coronado."

"Oh, shit. That reminds me. Coronado called this morning to say he is hosting a cocktail party this evening. Isn't Monday night a funny time for a party?"

"Not if you're into Monday night football?"

"It's Super Bowl time, Detective."

"NBA? WWF? Yeah, Coronado's worried about something!!"

"Thought, so." Cutty said with a smile.

Cynthia Marlee Preston

Chapter 37

**Monday, January 29, 2001
3:15 a.m.**

I woke up suddenly as the television went off the network. I had fallen asleep thinking about Randall as the guilty party. But a new thought now flashed into my head.

Maybe Cutty killed Bo? Why not? Maybe Bo had something on Cutty? It was common for family members to be suspects in a murder. Missing children are frequently the victims of abusive parents. I remember watching many newscasts of families crying together over the tragedy of their missing sons or daughters only to find out, months later that mother or father had confessed to the murder.

I had to admit that these were primarily white families. Black families seemed to have a different code when it came to blood. Besides that, I wondered about some of the unknowns in Cutty's past. Ellie confided in me that after Maggie was assaulted by the three thugs, the police found one of suspects and sent him to Stillwater Prison, for life. Two weeks later, he was found dead on the floor of the lower level of the recreational area. Apparently, he had slipped and fallen down a full flight of cement stairs. He died of head injuries.

Cutty was at home taking care of the children at the time, but Bo was serving six months in Stillwater on an assault charge. Bo called Cutty at Ellie's house to give him the news.

Ellie knew in her heart that Patrick had asked Bo to take care of the situation. It made her sick and satisfied, at the same time. After all, she was the one who had taken a leave of absence from work to nurse Maggie's slashed, broken and bruised body back to health.

There was also Dante who was dead himself but who could have killed Bo prior to his death. He would have had the same motive as Randall, fear of exposure, and it was no secret that Dante hated Cutty. Killing his brother might have made him feel vindicated for the fact that Cutty had moved in on his family while Dante was away trying to set up a future for them.

Being away from the cities and away from the men in my life made me feel whole again. I looked around the living room and noticed that everything looked especially sharp, crystal clear, watery bright, and shiny. I was in my zone, probably from the adrenaline pumping through my veins.

I had to make some choices.

"Look to the hands for the keys to the soul", the old lady in the dream had told me.

I looked at my own hands. They were chapped. I had had a hard time the last five years. My fingernails were short and my nail polish was chipped. I wore an engagement ring on my left hand with a cross on it and three diamonds. Cutty bought it for me for Christmas. I felt a calm come over me. My safe place again, within me, while without me was nothing but danger and lies.

It was at that moment that I took my final leap of faith with Cutty. I was going to trust him. I knew in my heart that Randall killed Bo.

What a strange world I was living in. A world where I could trust a man who had committed crimes for 7 years of his life more than I could trust a wealthy businessman like Randall. A world where my 15 year old daughter would be taken away from me by the system and put into the home of a murderer simply because his lifestyle appeared to be more respectable than mine.

A world where money and image rule and without money or image your struggles and sacrifice run paramount to your success. African Americans have no generations of wealthy ancestors from which to inherit land, goods or money, and they have a huge image problem with the white Anglo-Saxon Protestant majority.

With each passing generation the old ways fall to the new and some gain is made, but also with each passing generation some ground is lost by the majority rule of money loving and image driven whites who fear their dark skinned brothers because they know the power of the black man's spirit to overcome adversity. Successful black men have become successful in a variety of ways, including hopping on the white man's train, or by using their perfectly chiseled character to overcome adversity.

Character. A combination of ancient wisdom passed down and accepted as truth and the rock of faith in something greater than man.

Trust Cutty; believe that God is working out his perfect plan; put family first; and fight injustice.

Four cornerstones for me to focus on for the rest of my life.

I took a deep breath and slept like a baby the rest of the night.

Cynthia Marlee Preston

Chapter 38

**Monday, January 29, 2001
9:00 a.m. Lake Home**

Morning came quickly and sweetly to the lake. I opened my eyes and saw the sunlight dancing across the trees and flickering on silver snow banks leading down the embankment to the lake. There were no sounds of traffic or thumping stereos. Just the sounds of birds, squirrels and rabbits collecting their breakfast.

I was laying on the living room couch and looking out the huge glass picture windows that faced the lake. I needed to call Cutty but I had forgotten my cell phone at home, yesterday, when I went to pick up Shea. The lake home phone was disconnected for the winter and the nearest town was 20 miles away.

I got up and started a fire and turned on the news. Local news was on with a special report about the anti-government group that was holing up at the farmhouse on Lake George, about five miles northeast of here. The FBI had been arriving since last night and had now surrounded three sides of the compound. The fourth side was cut off by a lake but they were talking about bringing in a SWAT team on snowmobiles.

Every Secret Thing

The group was protesting an arrest of one of their leaders who was charged with income tax evasion. Excitement in the voices of the reporters reminded me of the small town living up here, where nothing much happens, except divorce and embezzlement. Basically, everyone believed that happiness could be achieved by getting more money or getting rid of a spouse.

I went outside and looked at the dark clouds moving in quickly. The chickadees were chattering and there were deer running through the back yard toward the woods behind us. By the look of the sky, I guessed the storm would be here by noon. The weatherman had said that we would have hazardous driving conditions by later this afternoon.

I walked down the big hill in front of the house that leads down to the lake. The lake, of course, was frozen and peppered with vacated ice fishing houses. It was Monday morning. There were beer cans surrounding most of the houses. Most were packed into plastic garbage bags and left, outside, as though a trash man would be coming along to collect them.

I found a house without a padlock and opened up the door. It was a typical Minnesota ice fishing house. It was wallpapered with Playmate of the Month foldouts and had a nice wood burning stove in the corner. I found myself a beer in the cooler and drank it. There were three chairs surrounding the hole, which had been augured into the ice. The ice looked like it was about three feet deep. Water splashed about inside the hole.

Two tackle boxes rested next to the chairs and a fish net hung on the wall. A radio sat on a small table, along with half-eaten chips and beer cans. Randall used to go ice fishing with his buddy, Mark. It was basically one more way for a white man to get out of the house on a Sunday afternoon. He would come back toe up and then have to go to work on Monday morning with a hangover. I suspected, by the number of beer cans, that there were several hung-over employees in town, today.

I was surprised that the owners of this house left it open. There was a padlock, but it wasn't locked. There was a pad of paper, a pencil and a deck of cards on the table, so I scrawled a note "Thanks for the beer! Terry." and left the house. I started my long journey walking across the lake.

This was my blood – this lake country. I could draw life from it like from no other earthly source. I had spent my teen-aged years coming to the cabin every summer. We were the rich kids, those of us who had enough money to own a home in Moorhead and a lake cabin on Pelican. We flaunted it, too. The kid with the biggest boat was top dog out here. The kid with the most lenient parents was second.

Every Secret Thing

Moorhead girls were superior to Fargo girls and Fargo boys were superior to Moorhead boys. Pelican Lake was the venue for rich Fargo and Moorhead teens to get together. I hung out with five other girls during the summer. We all had rich parents and were straight A students, cheerleaders and homecoming queen candidates during the school year at Moorhead Senior High School, but by summertime, we were the wild girls of Pelican Lake.

One night in July 1971, I snuck out with the boat at 1:00 a.m. I picked up Janet, Becky, Denise, Judy and Jean. They were all expecting me and waiting at the end of their docks for pick-up. Each had a bottle of liquor, stolen from their parents, and Janet had marijuana, stolen from her older brother.

We partied in the middle of the lake, on the boat, until 4:00 a.m., when Denise had the urge to go water skiing. We went to her dock and she picked up tow ropes and skis, enough for five of us to slalom. Judy was going to drive the boat because she couldn't get up on slalom, she had to drop a ski.

Becky stripped off her clothes and hopped into the chilly water. She was the best skier of us all. Janet, Denise, Jean and I stripped, too, and hopped into the water. We were all squealing and splashing each other. It was freezing!!

It took us three attempts before we all got up, but it was the most exciting moment of my life when the five of us were standing, totally nude, behind the boat, spraying each other as we cut back and forth across the wake. We never fell. We never wobbled. Judy brought us back to Denise's dock and five guys from Fargo were standing on the end of her dock. We squealed again, pulled ourselves into the boat and got dressed. They claimed that they got a picture of us with an infrared camera. I wonder, to this day, if that picture really exists. I would love to see it, if it does.

I looked down at my watch and it was already afternoon. I finished the walk around the lake and went home to make myself something to eat.

When I arrived, the Sheriff from Pelican Rapids was there. He asked me if everything was O.K. and I assured him that I was fine. I have never liked police officers. I would never confide in one. But now I knew that Cutty was worried about me, so I decided that I would drive into Pelican Rapids that evening and call him. I planned to leave for the Twin Cities in the morning. I was feeling much stronger and more at peace.

I made tacos and sipped on wine the rest of the day and evening, watching old movies on the VCR. It was about 10:00 p.m. when the doorbell rang. I couldn't believe that Randall and Shea were at the door. I opened it immediately. Shea ran over and hugged me.

"I guess a bad mother is better than no mother at all." Randall said as he walked in.

I wondered if he knew that he was quoting from *Gone with the Wind*. I doubted it.

I looked at Randall and noticed how icy blue his eyes were. A danger signal went up in my brain.

"Randall?", I asked, "can I get you some food?"

"No. We just ate on the way here."

I could tell he was drunk. Shea gave me the confirmation that I needed with her eyes.

"Randall," I said, "take a load off and relax in the recliner."

He dropped into the chair.

"What brings you up this way?" I asked.

"I had a delivery to make and I knew you would be here. Hear me out, Terry, now that I got Shea back you can come home, too, and we can be together again. I've come to take you back."

Cynthia Marlee Preston

Randall stumbled out of the chair and grabbed me and pulled me into the bedroom. Before I knew it he had pinned me to the bed with his body.

"How could you leave me for a nigger, Terry? How could you?" He screamed.

He slapped me hard across the face. Randall was thin, but he was 6'2" tall and I couldn't move. He punched my eyes and my lip. I could feel my lip bleeding. He started ripping my clothes.

Suddenly, from behind Randall's head, I could see Shea approaching with a golf club, a one wood. She lined up behind him and took a nice gold stance that Randall had taught her. She drew the club back, slowly, tipped her wrists and swung all the way through, knocking Randall out as the wood hit the back of his head.

"Fore", she cried.

I couldn't help but laugh.

"Fo Sho!!" I responded.

"C'mon, babe." I ordered and we ran out of the cabin and into my car, heading for Pelican Rapids.

Chapter 39

Monday, January 29, 2001
4:30 p.m.

Cutty buttoned up his Geoffrey Beene white cotton dress shirt with the French cuffs and fastened shut two gold and black opal cufflinks. He slipped on his black pin-striped vest and trousers and tied on a pair of Stacy Adams shoes.

He stood in front of the full-length mirror on the back of the bedroom door.

"Damn, Big C, you are looking GOOD tonight." He praised.

He put on his Christmas presents from Terry, a full-length black leather coat, a tan and black wool neck cover and a black wide-brimmed wool hat. He was satisfied with the fit and admired himself some more.

He still hadn't heard from Terry and he was growing increasingly concerned. Dectective Richards had called him about 2:00 to say that the Pelican Rapids police department had dispatched a squad car to check out the Onstad lake home, but he hadn't called back either.

Right now, Cutty's Capricorn spirit told him that he had business to handle and tonight Cutty was on point. He walked out the door and hopped into his Cadillac.

    The Coronado home was located on Lake Minnetonka, about 10 miles out on Hwy 12. This was the land of Minnesota's wealthiest musicians: Jimmy Jam and Terry Lewis; Prince was further out in Chanhassen. The estates on the lake were magnificent and Cutty was not quite prepared for what he was driving into that evening.

    The Coronado's Estate was at a fork in the road. Cutty had to drive several miles through woods to come to the gate. He had to pass through electronic security and a voice recognition system. Emilio must have taped their conversation yesterday, because the voice welcomed him by name and the gates were lifted.

    A valet met him at the door and took his car. Cutty flinched. Nobody had driven his car since he bought it. He let it go, but he watched it until it was out of sight.

    He straightened up his coat collar and entered the home. The entire foyer was filled with tropical gardens and waterfalls. He was led past the foyer to a huge receiving room where he took off his coat and hat and was asked to kindly remove his shoes. He was given a pair of house shoes and was taken into the lounge.

Emilio met him at the door of the lounge and directed him to a small group of men that he was conferring with prior to Cutty's entry. He introduced him to Peter Janz, Corporate Vice President of Jack Sprat Lowfat Chicken Products, Inc. and to Mike Bocco, Manager of Palace Shipping and Handling, Inc., and to Ross Lorentz, Attorney at Law. Each of the men nodded to Cutty as they were introduced. Each held his cocktail out as they nodded.

"Forgive me, Mr. Cutter, what will you be drinking tonight?"

"Hennessey" Cutty replied.

"Nice choice", Emilio replied and snapped his fingers.

"Yes, Sir?" The waiter responded to Emilio.

"Hennessey for my guest, Mr. Cutter."

"Yes, sir, very good" and then turning to Cutty asked "Will you have that neat or on ice?"

"Straight up." Cutty replied.

A tray of hors d'oeuvres came by and Cutty picked up a morsel of something brown, fumbling with his huge fingers to get it off the plate without touching all the others. He popped it into his mouth. It was something from the ocean, but he wasn't sure what. He chewed it once and swallowed. Salty, but good, he thought.

The Hennessey had arrived in a snifter and he washed down the salty fish with the whole snifter of Hennessey. The waiter looked puzzled for a moment and then regained his composure.

"I'll bring you another, Mr. Cutter, right away." He nodded and backed up.

"I like a man with a healthy constitution." Emilio said, and the other three men readily agreed.

"Now, Mr. Cutter. As we discussed on Saturday, we have a vacant position that we would like you to fill. But we also have a little trouble, right now. We think you can help us in a unique way." Coronado's voice was smooth and unruffled.

"You see, your fiancés ex-husband has been working with us in our northern territory, but he has recently been drawing some unwanted attention to himself. He is an emotional man and flares up, too easily. We got word, today, that Paul Richards, Minneapolis Homicide, is investigating him on the suspicion of the murder of your brother, Bo."

Cutty had to steady himself several times in that short conversation.

Every Secret Thing

First, the Hennessey hit him, then the revelation that Randall Onstad was working for Coronado, and finally that Randall had probably already murdered Bo and could now be on the way to the lake to murder Terry.

Cutty's second Hennessey arrived, but this time he just held it.

"Mr. Cutter. Have you ever done any damage control?" Emilio gave him that look that told him this was about a "hit".

"Yes", Cutty responded, shuffling side to side in a rocking motion that meant he was thinking very carefully about something.

"And, Mr. Cutter. Do you understand exactly to what I am referring?"

"Yes, I know what you mean, but how much are you willing to pay to make this worth my trouble?" Cutty stood stone still.

"You will be generously compensated, Mr. Cutter. We don't talk figures in the lounge. These three gentlemen will assist you if you need anything, or if there is any trouble."

"Just give me a call if you need storage." Mike Bocco said, handing Cutty his card.

"The VOICE—", Cutty grinned and pointed his finger at Mike, "the voice behind the light in the warehouse?"

"That's me." Mike replied, good naturedly.

"O.K., thanks man." Cutty said and then turned to the lawyer. He had seen this name on many envelopes that had come to the house.

"I do have one request of Mr. Lorentz." Cutty looked at him knowingly.

"No need for words, Mr. Cutter. We will make sure that Shea is put back into her mother's custody."

Cutty nodded.

"Shall we join the others for food, gentlemen?" Emilio asked of the others with his arms outstretched.

"You'll have to excuse me, Emilio. I have some preparations to attend to." Cutty told him.

"I understand, Mr. Cutter. We'll be in touch."

Cutty was escorted to the coat room and to the front door where the valet had his car warmed up and running. Coronado hadn't expected Cutty to stay. Very shrewd man, Emilio.

Cutty slapped a five dollar bill into the hand of a brother who had brought the car around.

"Now that's a Caddy!" He told Cutty.

"Thanks, man." Cutty replied while hopping in, and then stuck his head out the window.

"Hey, brother, does Emilio have a Lincoln?"

"No, way, man. Emilio is a Benz man."

"OK, thanks again, man."

"No problem."

Cutty checked to make sure his car was intact and then sped toward Coronado's gates.

Chapter 40

**Monday, January 29, 2001
7:00 p.m.**

Cutty had no intention of murdering Randall Onstad. He wasn't worth the bullet, or the risk, and he had no desire to go back to jail, but he was going to have to do some quick acting to get himself out of this mess with Coronado.

His first concern was for Terry's safety. He didn't know what Randall was capable of doing, now that he had killed once.

"Racist Mother-Fucking Asshole" he screamed into the windshield as he raced down Hwy 12 toward town. "You fucking killed my brother!!!"

Cutty's mind was racing, now. He picked up his cell phone and tried to call Terry's cell, again. Not turned on. "Damn it."

Cutty dialed Maggie's number.

"Yeah?"

"Nice phone manners, girl." He said.

"Fuck off." She laughed.

Maggie, do you still have the gun or did you bring her back to my mother, like I told you to do?"

"It's in my trunk."

"I figured as much. I'm coming by to get it. Stay where you're at."

He hung up the phone. He needed to swing by Maggie's house and then high-tail it to the cabin in the woods of northern Minnesota.

Chapter 41

Monday, January 29, 2001
7:30 p.m.

When Cutty got to Maggie's house, she insisted that he drive Darius's four-wheel drive pick-up truck. She had heard the weather reports on the winter storm raging throughout Minnesota. Darius wasn't too thrilled about the idea of lending his pick-up to Patrick Cutter, but he knew better than to argue with Maggie. Maggie was paying the bills.

Cutty grabbed some of his CD's out of the Cadillac, gave Maggie a hug and hopped into the truck. He drove north going 85 m.p.h. with blustering snow circling the highway and Snoop Dog rapping his smooth words: "What good is the truth if you can't tell a lie, sometimes."

Cutty road-tripped the distance in just under three hours. When he arrived, he walked into an empty lakehome. All of the lights were on, but after checking every room, he didn't see anyone.

There was a Lincoln Town Car in the driveway, but Terry's car was gone.

Cutty looked in the master bedroom and saw blood on the bedspread. He then grabbed the gun from his pocket and took off out the front door

Every Secret Thing

and down the hill to the lake. He could just barely make out the dark icehouses on the lake by the lights of the Onstad home. The sky was blue-black and snow was falling. He walked down to the lake and toward the icehouses.

Without knowing what else to do, he tried opening icehouse doors. The first two were padlocked shut. The third one was open. He pushed the door open and lit his lighter. Playboy centerfolds were hanging on all four walls.

He looked in the tackle box for a knife and found a filet knife. He put it in his coat pocket. When he looked at the table he saw the note that Terry had written to the icehouse owners. It was just like Terry to thank someone after helping herself to his beer. He grabbed himself a beer out of the cooler and drank the whole thing in one cold guzzle. He was relieved to know that Terry had been walking on the lake today. He prayed that she was still alive.

He left the Playboy icehouse and continued around the lake. From a distance he saw a house to the east with a light glowing. He snuck up on it and peeked in the window. The icehouse was full of crates marked "danger-explosives." Nobody was inside. Cutty moved around to the front door. There were three heavy-duty locks on the door.

He went back to the window and broke the glass out with his gun. He then climbed up into the icehouse through the window. Once inside, he shot the locks off of four differently marked crates. He discovered rifles, hand guns, grenades and dynamite.

Cutty heard a low volume engine sound in the distance. It was getting increasingly louder. He looked out of the window and saw the headlights of a snowmobile heading his way. He climbed out of the window and raced back to the Playboy house. He opened the door and saw Randall Onstad holding a golf club over his head. He brought it down hard on Cutty's head. Cutty dropped to the ice.

Randall picked up Cutty's gun and then searched his pockets and came up with the filet knife. He walked over to the ammunitions icehouse and met the snowmobile as it approached the icehouse.

The snowmobile pulled up and stopped. A large Cuban dressed in a one-piece thermal jumpsuit with a hood and ski goggles, got off and walked over to Randall.

"It's all there, guy. I just caught someone doing a little snooping, but everything is intact. Where is my fee?"

The Cuban handed Randall an envelope and proceeded to open all three padlocks with their respective keys. He pushed open the door and

Every Secret Thing

walked in. Randall followed. Assessing the size of the load he determined that it would take him several trips.

"How's everything going at the compound?" Randall asked.

"Not good. Our man is still in jail!! We will not tolerate the intrusion of the federal government into our homes and personal finances. Death to the IRS and all who support her!!! She is an evil she-bitch and must be destroyed. We will stay with our cause to the bitter end. Your timely delivery will improve our efforts. We still have access from the lake, but we were running out of ammunition."

"Great, I'm glad I could assist you." Randall said. "I'm going back up to my old lakehome to take care of some business. I'll be back next Monday with the next shipment."

"Thanks, comrade. United, we stand strong."

"United, we stand strong." Randall replied, preoccupied with more important matters. He then turned around and stalked off toward the Onstad lake home.

Chapter 42

**Monday, January 29, 2001
11:00 p.m.**

　　Randall walked across the frozen lake. His hat was covered with snow. He had a pocket full of cash, over $100,000 for this delivery because of the degree of danger in this situation; but, tonight there was no thrill when the money was handed to him. Usually, as he walked away after collecting his money, he would have a stiff cock from the thrill of the power, danger and money. Now he was thinking about the thrill of cutting Terry's throat and watching the blood push through the wound as her eyes showed her fear and pain.

　　"Terry! Daddy's home." He cried out into the night.

　　Randall wanted to kill Terry if he couldn't have her. His mental stability had crossed-over to the unstable side again, like the night he drove up Franklin and shot Bo Preston in the head. The nigger punk had threatened him with blackmail and had taken Stacy's car for a joy ride one evening. He found out because the police had ticketed it and called him as registered owner of the vehicle.

Every Secret Thing

Once he discovered where Stacy was living he went to visit her. When he saw the neighborhood he was shocked. Why would Stacy choose to live in the ghetto? Stacy was trying to keep something from him. He started snooping around and saw her with Dante one night. Once he discovered who she was involved with he decided to take his own action.

His daughters were the light of his life, and if he couldn't have them, no one else could. It was the same with Terry. No one else was going to have his first love.

Behind him he heard the hum of a snowmobile. Why was the comrade coming here? That was a breach of anonymity, damn it. But as the headlights got closer it looked like the damn thing was about to run him over.

Just as it was about to hit him, he jumped to the right and rolled over and over in the snow. The snowmobile hit the embankment, stopped for a moment and backed up. Randall started running up the hill. The snowmobile followed.

He ran around to the back of the house and into the shed. Terry's snowmobile was there, the door had been left open and the key was in the ignition. His very trusting ex-wife had just saved his life.

He opened the garage door to the shed, which gives access for the snowmobile to drive in and out of the shed. He fired it up and sped through the door and around to the front of the house. His assailant was close behind. He kicked it into full throttle and sailed down the hill to the lake. Once he hit the ice, he was sailing, almost lifted off the ice by the movement and the power.

The assailant caught up to him about three quarters of the way across the lake. He came along side of Randall, lifted up a rifle and shot at him. The shot nicked his handlebar and he felt the heat on his hand. What the hell was going on? Patrick Cutter was driving the damn snowmobile and shooting at him. He must have taken a rifle from the ammunitions icehouse. Shit.

Randall was scared, now. He headed back to the other side of the lake. If he could make it back home, he would take Cutter for a ride in the backwoods, behind the house and across the road. He knew that area like the back of his hand and could make his escape from there to the main road, going back to town.

He passed by the ammunitions icehouse and saw the Cuban lying still on the ice with a one wood golf club next to his head. Damn, one more birdie seeing stars tonight.

As he approached the lakeshore, he kicked the engine down a notch, for power. He flew up

Every Secret Thing

the hill while Cutty had slowed down on the embankment. Randall sailed around the house and toward the woods. He went down a hill to enter the wooded lot that he and Terry had owned together for 20 years. Cutty was on his tail. Another shot rang out. This one missed.

Just then a large buck bounded out from his hiding spot and stopped dead in the path that Randall was traveling. Randall turned a sharp right, almost rolling the ski-doo. He made that turn on one ski. He looked back and saw Cutty make the same smooth turn as he. He watched the buck bound away, untouched.

Randall needed a quick plan. His adrenaline was kicking in and he was thinking very clearly. There was an opening just south a short distance where the deer liked to graze. From there he would be able to get to the main road but there was an electronic fence separating the Onstad property from the main road. He didn't know if he would be able to break through. Damn. Maybe he could set it up so that he would turn at the last minute and Cutty would hit the fence.

He started weaving back and forth through trees and branches and ground brush. Cutty was right at his back but was using both hands to drive and hadn't fired again.

Randall arrived at the opening. Ok, ready, steady Randy, boy. He was headed straight for the fence and then he turned the most magnificent quick left that he had every maneuvered.

"YES!" He screamed out into the cold silent night. "Adios, Nigger!"

Two seconds later, Cutty slammed into the electronic fence and the entire snowmobile lit up in smoke and flames as Cutty was thrown from the seat, his clothes on fire, sailing across the fence and landing on his back in the snow by the main road.

"Were having dark meat tonight, charcoaled just the way you like it, Terry." He said out loud, laughing hysterically.

Randall drove his snowmobile back to the shed but saw that Terry's car was parked in the driveway, now. He quietly maneuvered around the Anderson's house to the left and down to the lake. There he got off the machine.

With complete focus and forethought, Randall walked up the embankment to the house. This was his house, damn it, before the divorce. He was excited to confront Terry and make her squirm for a while before he shot her. Then, he was going to look down on her and watch the life drain out of her face.

He walked in the front door and saw Terry and Shea standing in the kitchen. He pointed the gun toward Terry.

"Terry?" he asked as he looked me.

"What?" I replied.

"Don't you understand that I am the only one who can take care of you? You need me. You can't live without me. You'll wind up in hell, without me!!"

"Yes, Randall. I think I understand now. Now hand me the gun."

"Get on your knees, BITCH, and beg God for forgiveness."

Terry dropped to her knees. The police officer from Pelican Rapids came around the fireplace and Randall turned quickly, fired off a shot and hit him in the forehead.

Terry and Shea screamed, and closed their eyes. Randall was aiming at them, now.

A shot rang out, and all of the glass blew out of the sliding glass doors that gave view to the lakeshore side from the front of the house. Glass sprayed everywhere. A second shot rang out. Terry grabbed Shea by the shoulders and pulled her to the ground behind the kitchen counter.

When Terry heard the sound of the glass stop shattering she looked out and watched Randall fall to the floor, shot clean from the back of the head.

Cutty stood on the porch. He was filthy with mud, blood and his clothes were burnt in places, but he stood erect and focused, holding a rifle at his side.

It took a few moments for Terry to understand that Randall was dead and Cutty was alive.

Terry walked over to Randall and bent to her knees. Shea sobbed and hugged her mother. Cutty came over and pulled them all together and hugged them with his big arms.

"What it's come to..." Cutty said, and broke out into uncontrollable sobs. "My, God, what has it come to..."

Chapter 43

Tuesday, January 30, 2001
4:00 p.m.

Cutty, Shea and I arrived back in Minneapolis about 4:00 Tuesday afternoon. We stopped at Maggies' house to exchange Darius's car for Cutty's Caddy.

As Shea and I revealed the sensational story to Maggie, Cutty thanked Darius for the use of his vehicle and for taking care of Maggie.

"You keep her ass at home in bed with you, only," he said "or I'll be paying you a visit that ain't gonna be pleasant, you hear, bro?"

"Yeah, I hear ya, but it ain't gonna be easy!"

"Nothing worthwhile ever is easy. Get used to it."

He slapped Darius on the back and we left. Cutty drove home and dropped off Shea and me. He told me he had one more errand to run and that I should take a hot bath and get ready for him!!!

Cutty drove off and headed for Hwy 12. About 45 minutes later he pulled up to the Coronado gates and was let in. He met with Coronado in his study and received a check for $750,000. He left as calmly as he arrived, but just as he got to the door, Coronado summoned him.

"Mr. Cutter? You're a lucky man. May I call you again if I need you?"

"You may call, but it will be up to me to decide if I need you, Emilio."

Emilio laughed.

"So be it, Cutty. So be it".

About the Author

Cynthia Preston, 47, lives with her husband, Patrick in Moorhead, Minnesota where she is the Assistant Vice President for Academic Affairs at Minnesota State University Moorhead. Cynthia and Patrick have eleven children between them; Phillip, Stephanie (Stevie), Natasha, Samantha, Angelina (Butter), Patrick (Junior), Nicolle, Sophia, Isaiah, Leonard (L.P), and Elijah. Patrick's son, Stephen, would have been 10 years old this year, but was taken at 4 months by SIDS.

Cynthia was raised in Moorhead but has spent the majority of her adult life in the Twin Cities where she was the registrar at Metropolitan State University. She recently returned to her hometown. She enjoys golf, bowling, reading, writing and playing with her two pre-school children. Her two older daughters, Stevie and Sam Olson, and her two young children Sophia and LP Rummels are the sunlight of her life.

Printed in the United States
715100002B